BLADES OF THE BANISHED
BOOK FOUR OF THE RAITHLINDRATH SERIES

Robert Ryan

Cover Design by www.ebooklaunch.com

ISBN-13 978-0-9942054-1-4
(print edition)

Trotting Fox Press

Contents

1. I See a Dark Tower

Lanrik watched patiently, but he did not like what he saw.

A cold breeze blew through the night, cutting across a dry and weathered land. It brought dust; the same powdery grime that had coated his boots, clothes and face for days. He tasted it in his throat. Or maybe that was fear.

He looked at Erlissa. The breeze tugged at the fringe of her hair, tossing thick strands before her eyes. She made no move to flick them away. She could not.

The flurry died, and the dust settled. Erlissa's hair fell still. From afar, he caught the scent of cedar. The crisp smell was fresh and full of life.

Southward, the brooding shape of the Graèglin Dennath mountains bulked against the starry night. The cedar trees grew on their high and remote slopes. The final destination of their quest was somewhere among them, but that did not concern him now.

He curled a finger behind the lock of Erlissa's hair and gently pulled it clear of her eyes. She had not moved for minutes. Placing a cheek near her mouth, he sensed no breath from her lips. Nor did he see any rise and fall of her chest. He felt her skin and found it cold.

But she had warned him of those things.

The trance was her idea, and he had begrudgingly agreed. It was nothing that she had learned from Aranloth. It was her seeker sense, the gift that she was born with that allowed this. But the lòhren had taught her other skills, and she blended them now, using them

3

to delve deeper into her natural talent than she had ever done before. For to save Aranloth, they must not only seek out where his enemies held him captive, but also how. Assuming, of course, that he was still alive.

While they journeyed southward from the tor to the Graèglin Dennath, she had done the same thing several times. On each occasion the effort taxed her more. But the closer she approached the clearer her visions became. They now knew Aranloth's location in the mountains. What they needed was a better vision of his surroundings, of those who held him captive and their means of doing so. Only with that knowledge could they hope to form a plan of rescue.

Her chest heaved for sudden breath. Her crossed legs, on which she sat, twitched. Then her eyes flicked open, but her gaze was distant as though she did not see him.

Yet still she spoke.

"I see the land," she said. "It is barren. The bones of the earth stand tall. The mountains rise steep. Their jagged peaks, sharp like teeth, pierce the cold of the high airs. Wind shrieks over ridges and moans in the gaping mouths of ancient caves."

She paused, and her body shuddered. Her eyes darted left and right, but they saw nothing of the camp where Lanrik sat and watched nervously. He reached out to hold her hand, and she latched onto him.

"I see dust and smoke in the air. And ash so fine that it barely exists. Yet it chokes my throat and burns. It burns like the sun, and the clouds, as though they are red shrouds, blaze in wind-blown trails across the fiery sky."

As though in answer to her strange words, the breeze stirred again. Now, it blew from a different mountain and Lanrik smelled fumes and sulfur.

Erlissa paused, her breath ragged as she gasped at the dry air. But when she continued, her voice was calmer.

"I see smoke riding the wind, and white ash layering the barren ground. Rock and sand and withered grasses lie under a choking blanket. Everywhere is … despair. It is a dying place, full of misery. The land groans. Jutting from the mountains is a ragged peak. It thrusts its head above the clogging pall. It draws me. The land flows like a river. High runs a winding path. Far up the mountain's shoulder is a ridge. Atop the ridge stands a tower – tall and dark and grim, made of black stone, dull and void of light like long-dead embers."

Erlissa drew a deep breath. The air whistled in her throat.

"Long-forgotten sorcery hangs over the mountain like slow-drifting fog. It slumbers, quiet and restful, on the breast of oblivion. Yet still it might waken, if I am not careful. It is everywhere. The place reeks of it. And of death. And the tower is the beating heart of the age-old darkness."

Lanrik wished he could help. But he felt powerless. Conhain's sword hung at his side, useless to him. Yet, he still wanted to draw it. More than anything he felt a sudden desire to be something greater than a Raithlin. Greater than a Lindrath. He ached to be with her, to help her, but that was impossible, and it scared him.

"I see a closed door at the tower's base," she continued. "But it is blocked by rubble. The pinnacle is broken, like a tree with a destroyed crown. Merlons, battlements, mighty slabs of stone have all fallen from the turret."

She hesitated. Lanrik saw a pulse in her neck twitch and throb to the beat of her racing heart.

"No!" she said suddenly. "Not fallen. Not toppled by time, but *cast*. It is no accident. It bars entrance to the tower by design."

Her eyes widened, as though straining to see. "Yes. I approach. The top of the tower draws me. It pulls me, and I come."

Her voice stilled. A moment she ceased to breathe. And then she spoke again.

"I see ... Aranloth. He sits on the bare stone. His robes shimmer in the starlight, blazing white against the black flooring. The stars wheel above. The hot sun roves the sky. He moves little, nursing his strength during the baking days, shivering through the bitter nights, for he has nothing to eat and only nighttime dew from cold stone to sustain him. His fingers move, drumming against his staff. But now, now he stirs. He raises his head tiredly. He looks around. He looks straight at me. No! Not now. My sight blurs. The vision is gone!"

Erlissa paused. The skin of her hand was cold and clammy in Lanrik's.

"No, it is not gone," she said. "Now I see elùgroths, dim and dark, their wych-wood staffs gripped in pallid hands beneath the stars. They sit in a wedge below the tower, far enough away to avoid attack by lòhrengai and stone. They bend their will to one purpose. They strive, working in unison to bring the building down. Their minds encircle its ancient foundations, probing them, seeking weaknesses, straining to break and sunder. Now, now I see Aranloth again. He trains the force of his iron-like will upon the same foundations ... resisting. One man against many. Day after day, night after night. He is strong, but they are many. And ... *he* is among them. Elù-Randùr."

Erlissa spoke the last words with dread. Her head moved from side to side and her skin paled further. Lanrik would have woken her had she not warned him against doing so. He considered it anyway.

6

"Aranloth!" she said suddenly. "His face is so weary. His eyes so sad. But hope is still there, though it ebbs low. He looks up at me. He shakes his head. 'No,' he mouths. 'Flee!' he commands in the silence of the void. And he is gone."

Erlissa gripped Lanrik's hand with unexpected force. He did not know she possessed such strength.

"I see more," she said. "There is … something else." She took a deep breath and then spoke slowly. "The way is dark. Dark beneath the bones of the earth. And *something* …" she paused long seconds. "No, I am too weak. The vision slips away."

A few moments she remained as she was, and Lanrik watched anxiously. As he did so, a spasm racked her body, causing her arms and legs to stiffen, and her muscles to harden and bulge. Her eyes did not blink, and her strange gaze cut straight through him as though he was not there.

He felt panic rise. She was delving into arts that she was not ready for. He knew that much, even if he did not understand them. He knew also that she had held something back. She had seen more than her words had revealed, but he had no time to think on it.

She shuddered again and whispered. *I won't abandon him.* And then she toppled from her cross-legged position. Her staff fell from her grip and rattled against the dry earth.

He felt for a pulse, and found one, but it skipped beneath his fingers, thready and weak. Her clothes were damp with sweat, and her skin blue and cold.

Taking her wrists in his hands, he began to rub them, but that would not get the warmth back into her. Not quickly enough, and he knew that he needed to do more. Fire was required, and yet here, in the open lands of their enemies, flame was not their friend. It could draw any number of foes to their camp.

He sat for a moment, undecided. And then he made his choice. Without fire, she would likely die. He would take the risks it brought and be ready, as best he could, for any consequences.

A quick search of the campsite revealed dry grass, brittle twigs and dead bushes. He piled them up carefully, placing the finest material at the bottom and working up to the larger items. The sparks from his tinderbox caught quickly and soon flames sprang to life. He added more material as it burned.

A homely fire flickered in the night before him. It would be visible for miles though, and the dry bushes gave off thick smoke that would travel far through the air.

He rubbed her skin again, keeping her as close to the heat as he could without her clothes catching alight.

She had risked her life just now to help Aranloth, and by lighting the fire to save her, he was risking his own. Aranloth, in his turn, would do the same for either of them. He had proved it in the past. Lanrik shrugged to himself. *Those we love the deepest bring us the greatest pain.*

The fire smelled good. Color returned to Erlissa's skin, and her pulse steadied. He let her sleep. She needed rest, both to recover from forcing a vision, something that he had never even seen Aranloth do, and for the dangerous days ahead.

He did not doubt that this last time she had found Aranloth's exact location. But knowing that was only half of what was needed. Getting him out would be the next part, and from what Erlissa had said, strange though her words were, that sounded even harder than they had guessed. A wedge of elùgroths, including Elù-Randùr, was not only beyond their strength, but also beyond any subterfuge that he could think of.

The night wore on. He dozed fitfully, but kept a careful eye on the horses. Their senses were keener than his own, and they would alert him to the presence of anyone come to investigate the fire. To his relief, they remained quiet.

His gaze lingered frequently on the third horse. It was the embodiment of optimism: they had brought it for Aranloth. But getting the lòhren into its saddle was going to be hard. He had no doubt of that, and likely enough, all three horses would soon acquire new owners.

He pulled his Raithlin cloak tighter and dismissed that line of thinking. There was no future in it. Success never came from dwelling on what could go wrong. That must be acknowledged, but never allowed to dominate.

He saw no way to rescue someone from the midst of sorcerers – but that did not mean that a way did not exist. He would not give up. Aranloth needed him. And Alithoras needed the lòhren. He and Erlissa would find a way to do what they had come for. Or at least, they would devise a plan that maximized their chances of success. Being overly optimistic was just as sure a route to failure as pessimism.

The hours passed. Erlissa continued to sleep, and he allowed the fire to burn down to white ashes. He did not think she needed the warmth anymore.

He woke out of a doze and looked straight to the horses. Their ears were pricked and they seemed agitated. He cursed under his breath but wasted no time drawing his sword. The great blade of Conhain felt good in his grip, and that made him surer of himself.

He listened, but heard nothing.

One of the horses picked at some dry stubble, but the other two remained as they were, heads high and ears swiveling.

Lanrik strained to see beyond the rim of the camp. He detected no movement. Nor could he hear anything. Perhaps the horses had merely caught a scent that they did not like; a wolf or some other nighttime prowler of this foreign land.

On the other hand, the prowlers might be of the two-legged kind: Azan or elugs. This was their home, after all, and though it was a vast and empty place, it was not so forsaken that unfriendly eyes could not have seen the fire.

He stood. Stepping with care, he moved to the perimeter of the camp. He made little noise, but if someone was there, they had likely seen him already.

The night was dark. The sound of the breeze running through the dry seed-heads of the sparse grass smothered whatever slight noises he made.

He could not be sure that someone was out there, but he had to investigate. He edged his way around the outside of the camp. The ground was mostly hardened dirt, and he saw nothing until he came to a patch of loose sand. There, even in the dim light, he spotted a clear boot track.

It was not his own, nor Erlissa's. Casting his searching gaze about, he soon saw others. They were of a type that he had come across before. The stride was ungainly. The tracks deep. The boots iron-shod. Undoubtedly, they were left by the enemies that he most feared: elugs.

He stood a moment, paused in thought. Even as he studied one of the imprints its sharp edge collapsed, the dry sand falling into the deep indentation of a heel.

The tracks were fresh, only minutes, perhaps even seconds old. The knowledge sent a chill up his back and prickled the hair on his neck.

2. The Hunted

Lanrik turned and sprinted back to Erlissa. Gripping her shoulder, he shook her awake. He feared she would be dazed, but she came out of her trance-induced stupor with clarity.

"*Elugs*," he whispered urgently.

He did not need to say more. She reached out and took hold of her staff. Using it to help her, she tottered to her feet.

They stood there for a second, their gaze searching the darkness outside the rim of their camp. The bright blade of Conhain glittered beneath the stars.

From their left, a whistling sound broke the silence and a dark shape flashed through the air near them. It was an arrow.

Lanrik took Erlissa's hand and together they dived to the ground a few paces away. There was little cover there, merely an outcrop of rock barely a foot high and a dozen wide. But a crack ran down its center, and it offered some protection from all sides. They would make do with it.

The horses were not far away, but the empty space between was a killing ground. No matter how fast they ran they could never reach them, let alone saddle them, without being cut down by arrows.

There would be more than one elug, but their enemies had only fired one arrow. That gave him hope. It seemed there were not so many that they wanted to storm the camp, and perhaps only the one archer.

They waited. It was hard and uncomfortable where they were, but it seemed to provide enough cover that the archer could not see a target. Lanrik looked at the horses. It was not safe to raise his head very high, but he needed to keep an eye on them and watch that the other elugs did not change their mind and charge the camp.

He heard another arrow wing through the night. He ducked his head and the shaft smashed into the rock several feet away. Wood shattered and shards flew everywhere.

He cursed, but saw nothing for it but to wait. They could not reach the horses, nor could they abandon them. Not in this land so far from home, and especially not with the task of saving Aranloth that they had set themselves. If they managed to do it, they would need to escape quickly.

And yet, he realized grimly, to wait was only to put off the inevitable. The elugs already knew that. Come daylight, he and Erlissa would be in a worse plight. Their attackers had not ventured into the camp for that reason. If the archer could not pick them off in the dark, he would have a better chance during the day. Not only that, a runner had likely been sent for reinforcements. When they came, swords would accomplish whatever arrows had not.

Lanrik studied the night and made his choice. The hunted must turn into hunter. He whispered his intentions to Erlissa. Fear gleamed in her eyes, but no refutation came to her lips. She understood the situation, and she trusted his Raithlin skills.

He slowly slipped out from the crack of rock and onto the barren ground near the edge of the camp. He hoped those skills were enough. What he did now was perhaps the most dangerous part of his plan. Once free of the campsite, he would be able to move more freely and choose the best cover that the sparse land allowed. At the moment, with the archer's eyes no doubt seeking out any sign of movement, he might easily be seen.

But he took care to avoid that. He moved in the opposite direction to the horses, for the elugs would anticipate, if anything, a dash toward them. Using the Raithlin crawl, he inched ahead so slowly that there was barely any progress, yet to move faster was to risk being seen. And though his progress was slow, after many long minutes, he neared the edge of the camp.

He kept so low to the ground that he was able to utilize even the slightest of depressions to help break up his outline, as well as the variations of soil color and texture that he found.

Near the edge of the camp was a patch of dry grass, which he avoided, as there was no chance of moving through it without noise. It took longer, but eventually he circled the area, and having done so, was now out of the camp.

Erlissa was by herself, and he was now out in the night, but he was not safe. He did not know where the elugs were: either in one main group or spread around the camp. He must find out, and in finding out, put into action his plan.

He stood up, using a waist high bush to help break his outline, and stalked with great care ahead into the dark. He did not want to circle the camp yet. Instead, he moved further away until he was beyond the likely position of any elugs. Only then did he change direction.

He did not go far before he saw the first elug. It took a long while for his eyes to pick out the details in the dark, but from time to time the elug moved, and on each occasion Lanrik got a clearer picture.

It was by itself, stretched out on the ground and facing the camp. It held a drawn scimitar loosely in its hand.

Lanrik memorized the twisted and misshapen bush beside it, and let the creature be. He wanted to know where the others were, and how many of them there were, before he attempted anything. Most of all, he wanted to know where the archer was.

The minutes passed and Lanrik edged away. Soon, he saw others. He left them alone too. Some stood, but most lay down. All, however, gripped their swords and focused inward on the camp.

He smiled in the dark. They knew he was close; it was just that they thought him pinned down within their area of scrutiny and not behind them. If they knew that, they would jump to their feet and race for the hills with pounding hearts.

It was not these elugs who worried him. He was nearly all the way around to the other side before he saw the archer. It was the bow that gave him away. The elug who bore it was well concealed, standing in the deep shadows of a tall bush, but he had a habit of shifting the weapon from hand to hand.

Lanrik hardened himself. He knew what he had to do, even if he did not like it. The bow was a tool that gave the elugs an advantage. He must remove that assistance, and take it for himself. There was only one way to do that.

He drew one of his knives. He held it by the hilt, but bent his wrist upward to conceal the blade behind his arm. Even the slightest glint of starlight on metal was dangerous.

The night wore on. He could not see Erlissa, which was just as well. He could not even see the slab of rock in which she hid, but the elug, being closer, would have a better view.

He was close now. Close enough that he could see the elug breathe. He saw the clothes he wore, even detected something of their colors. He noted the bulge of different knives from various sheaths, and saw a hint of the creature's gray-tinged skin. He could not see its face, and that was just as well.

A moment he stood there, unwilling to do what he must. It was a moment of hesitation that lasted too long. By some sense, or perhaps by ill chance, the elug turned and looked back. The creature's eyes widened in fear, and he made as though to yell.

Lanrik was already moving. With great force he threw the knife. It streaked through the air and took the creature in the throat. There was a heavy thump. The elug started to scramble away, but Lanrik was on him. He pushed him down and covered his mouth. A few moments only the elug thrashed beneath him, but he bled out swiftly and died. Lanrik retrieved the bow, ignoring the blood that covered both of his hands as well as the side of his Raithlin cloak.

Quickly, he undid the elug's quiver and hung it over his own shoulder. Then he moved, swiftly as he dared, back into the shadows and away from the camp.

It was not the silent kill that he had hoped for. He expected some of the others to come and investigate, but he heard and saw nothing. It seemed as though they had not noticed any noise, or had not realized its import.

While he waited he reached back and used his fingers to count the arrows in the quiver. There were thirteen left. Not many, but perhaps enough to make all the difference in the world.

He started to move around the camp again. In a while, he was where he had first come out, and began to look for the twisted and misshapen bush where he had seen the first elug.

The creature was no longer there. Lanrik paused in mid-step. He had not expected it to move, and in truth, he saw no reason for it, unless it had heard the killing of its companion but was slow to investigate. If so, what would it do?

Lanrik hesitated. He did not move, aware that death was in the dark all around him. What would he do in the other's place? First, he would go to where the noise came from, but if he was suspicious, and he would be, he would not take the direct route. Instead, he would ease back to somewhere near where he was now, and circle around at a distance.

The hair stood up on the back of his neck. If so, the elug was near. Very near. He did not think it had made it further around toward the body, otherwise he would have encountered it already.

He was caught. If he moved to put down the bow, useless to him at close quarters, in order to draw his sword, the elug would see him. Assuming that he had not already done so.

He thought about that. If so, why had the elug not acted? He need not attack. A few shouts would bring at least some of his companions.

Lanrik considered the situation. It was torture to stand still and take no action, all the while aware that his enemy was somewhere close, but what he needed to do most was think.

If the elug took no action, it was because he did not know anybody was there. So far so good. That meant he was still investigating, making his way toward the noise of the first killing. If so, he would move again—

Just at that moment Lanrik heard a noise. It came from further out of the camp than he was, perhaps a dozen paces away. He slowly turned his head in that direction.

He saw nothing, but continued to watch, ever so slowly reaching up for an arrow from the quiver. He had drawn a shaft from the sheath but not nocked it when he finally saw the elug. It too was standing, and it stepped out slowly again in the direction that Lanrik had come from.

Movement, always the greatest risk in these circumstances, had given the creature away. It was undoubtedly on its way to investigate the previous noises, but must have heard or sensed him and paused. But not noticing anything further now thought it safe to continue. That was a mistake.

In a smooth motion Lanrik nocked the arrow, drew the bow and sent the shaft hurtling through the night.

There was a thud and muffled cry. The elug went down, an arrow fixed through its throat. It was a risky shot, for the neck was a difficult target in the dark even at close range, especially with a bow he was not familiar with, but a body shot would not have given him the instant kill that he needed.

Lanrik dropped to the ground and used the Raithlin crawl to get out of the area. He did not know if these new noises would draw more elugs. Nor did he know if he had given away his position when moving swiftly to fire the bow. Either way, he had to move to another point.

He still felt the blood on him from the first elug, and he did not like it. He did not like this killing in the dark, this sending of death through the air to an enemy who never saw it coming. Yet the elugs had attacked first, and beyond any doubt would kill him and Erlissa the moment they got the chance. He did what was necessary, but that did not mean he liked it.

As he crawled he came unexpectedly face to face with another elug doing the same. They were so close that even in the dark he could see its surprise. He must have shown the same astonishment. The elug reacted quicker though, for it held a sword ready in its hand. It stood and swung wildly, putting the weapon to instant use.

Lanrik dropped the bow and reeled back, coming to his feet awkwardly. It was just enough. The flashing blade of his foe passed within an inch of his face. He staggered back another pace, and now Conhain's sword was in his hand.

He attacked. This was a fight that he must win in seconds or risk others joining the fray.

The elug retreated in the face of swift blows, but it managed to get its scimitar up and block them. Steel on steel rang through the night. And then there was a scream as Lanrik thrust forward, driving his blade deep in the elug's belly and up toward its heart.

He ripped the blade free, bent down and grabbed the bow, and then stood frozen for half a second deciding what to do next.

Elugs would rush here to see what was happening, and he had no desire to face them. He had retrieved the bow, which was his main aim, and counted the number of enemies: ten in total, now reduced to seven. It was time to get back into the camp and rejoin Erlissa, unseen if he could manage it. Let the elugs make of the noises and their dead comrades what they could.

He risked moving away without using the Raithlin crawl. Instead, he ran through the dark, considering that the way he had come was free of elugs; he had killed the closest ones in that direction.

So it proved to be, for he reached the point where he had originally exited the camp without incident, although within moments he heard noses from all around in the dark.

He rested a few seconds, getting his breath back and cleaning the blade as best he could, wiping the blood from it onto the back of his trousers. There was nothing else to use.

He sheathed the blade, for nothing would give him away quicker than the glint of metal in the dark.

Using the Raithlin crawl again, he moved in toward the camp. He circled the patch of dead grass, moving quicker than he had on the way out. There was no archer this time to pick him off. Still, he did not want to be seen by the elugs. Let them fear that their enemies were outside, as well as inside the camp, and that there were more than two to deal with.

He paused. A muffled noise came from somewhere behind him, but it was not close. Soon there was another and he heard whispering voices. That too soon stopped. They were bound to stumble across at least one of the dead elugs. While they wondered what it all meant, he made his way back into the camp.

He reached the cracked slab of stone, and Erlissa rose up, ready to strike him with her staff, but just as quickly ducked down again and out of sight when she saw it was him.

He slipped back into the crack with her. She looked at him. He saw her gaze fall to the bow and her realization of what that meant. At least one elug was dead at his hands, perhaps others. But her look was one of relief. *He* was still alive.

She leaned in close and whispered. "What now?"

3. That which Lies Beyond

Erlissa did not seem surprised when she heard his whispered plan. She was used to the way he thought. In truth, he supposed, his methods had become part of her own way of thinking. Just as hers were becoming part of his.

She got ready quickly, took a deep breath, and then raced toward the horses. At the same time, he leaped atop the slab of stone. It offered a good vantage point to see the whole camp, especially aided by the light that now flared at the tip of her staff.

Startled shouts from beyond the camp broke the quiet, and then, as expected, the elugs raced in. Their drawn swords gleamed wickedly in the lòhren-light, but Erlissa paid them no heed. Instead, she started saddling the horses.

Lanrik, an arrow already set to the string, drew his bow and felled the first into the camp. There was little noise except for the quick whistle of fletching, and then a heavy thud. But the other elugs had seen what was done. Instead of support from their own archer, they were now under fire from the enemy.

They hesitated. And in that time Lanrik drew and loosed another arrow. This one was not a clean strike. It took the elug through his shoulder. A painful wound, and dangerous if infection set in, but not a killing one. However, it was enough.

The elugs were now reduced to five able-bodied warriors, and they did not like their chances. They turned and fled into the dark.

Whether they left completely, or lurked nearby trying to summon the courage for another attack, Lanrik did not know. He stayed where he was, poised and alert, while Erlissa continued to ready the horses.

When she was done, she mounted and looked over at him.

He had ten arrows left. Placing the nocked arrow back in the quiver, he counted them again, for it was vital to be sure of such things. He then drew his sword and strode to his horse.

Erlissa held onto the lead rope of the third mount, allowing Lanrik to keep his sword arm free. She then extinguished the light of her staff, and they trotted off into the night.

They kept up a good pace. Should there be another attack it would happen soon. But they saw no sign of the elugs, and as the minutes wore on they knew their enemies were now well behind them. At least, that particular group.

"Word of our presence will spread," Lanrik said. "We'd better be even more careful from now on, because they'll be searching for us."

"At least one thing is in our favor – they don't know where we're going."

"That's true." Lanrik said. He paused, and then spoke again. "But what of us. Do *we* know exactly where we're going?"

"Yes. I can feel the place even now. I could find my way there blindfolded." She raised her staff and pointed to the dim outline of several mountains ahead. "We go there. My seeker senses didn't fail me. Up that way is a long valley. Peaks crowd its sides, but we seek the highest one. If I close my eyes, I can see Assurah's tower, which stands in its shadow, all dark and grim against the starry sky."

They spoke no more for a while. Lanrik wanted to travel as far as they could to get away from any immediate search. The pounding of hooves was loud, and the horses kicked dust up into the cool night air.

The mountains loomed ahead, and the land they rode already sloped upward steeply. They were no doubt leaving tracks that the elugs could follow, but he would soon make it harder for them.

Up in the mountains there were many ways to hide their trail, for the terrain varied more frequently and there would be, at least he expected there would be, less sand and more rock. He would use every trick he had, and every nuance of the landscape, to help him. He did not think the elugs would be able to follow them for long.

They rode through the night. Their enemies were behind them, though what elugs or Azan might be ahead, they did not know. For that reason they took their time and went slowly and quietly to ensure they did not stumble into anything unexpected.

After many miles they came to a dry riverbed. How long since water had flowed down its course, Lanrik could not guess. But once water had gauged a path, cutting through earth and rock alike. Rounded stones formed the bed rather than sand, and that would help hide their trail. A Raithlin would be able to follow them without trouble, but he doubted any of the elugs had that skill. Of the Azan, he was less sure.

Now that Erlissa knew more of Aranloth's captivity, it was time to talk.

"What of Aranloth?" he asked. "Do you think we can break him free?"

"Maybe," she answered. "We knew before coming here that it would be difficult, though."

"Yes, but difficult is one thing, and impossible is another. I'm not suggesting we turn around, but from what you described of your vision, well, let's just say it didn't give me much hope."

Erlissa shrugged. "This is not a land for hope. But I think it can be done. The way is not … clear, though. There are too many elùgroths, and they are beyond my power. If they could be defeated, Aranloth would already have done so. He and I together would have a better chance. But even then, I think not. We must find a way that does not involve direct confrontation."

Lanrik knew she already had something in mind. There was more to her vision than she had revealed.

"What other way is there?" he asked.

"Oh, there's at least one other way. But it's nearly as dangerous, even if they would not expect it. We have to think of something else. The other … possibility is a last resort."

He did not press her for more details. He sensed once again that she was reluctant to talk about it. That did not bode well for whatever it was, and by the sounds of it, it offered only a marginally better chance than challenging the elùgroths directly. He was not sure that he wanted to know more about such an option.

He changed the subject. "It's strange to think that the shazrahad sword came from somewhere near here. This land is so different from Esgallien. I feel like I don't belong here, as if the land itself hates me. I wonder if elugs and Azan feel that way when they come north?"

"I expect so," Erlissa answered. "But the sword did not just come from somewhere in this area. Assurah forged it here, on the very mountain that we now climb. His presence, and the lingering remnants of his sorcery, are all about us – even after all this time. Truly, the land reeks of him and his works." She frowned. "And I can

24

sense something familiar too. The sword spent years beyond count in this place. The tower that I described, the dark one, is where he forged it."

Lanrik considered that "It's no accident then that Aranloth came here. I wonder if he found out anything about the sword?"

Erlissa grinned at him. "You can ask him, once we break him free."

Lanrik admired her optimism, or at least her ability to make light of the situation. It was strange, though. When first they met she was not like that at all. She had changed. Or becoming a lòhren had changed her. Or maybe something else. Whatever the cause of it, she was becoming more like him. At least, his old self. But he knew that he was changing too. A man could not go through what he had and remain the same. He was picking up more of her nonchalant attitude. What would be would be. He still planned though. He would *always* plan. Just like he wanted to think of a strategy now to save Aranloth. He knew it was too early for that though. They still needed more information, and he must see this tower for himself, first.

Dawn came at the end of a long night. Smoke hung in the air. The sky glowered red and fiery. Through all the dark hours they had climbed high, and Lanrik knew they had always headed upward, but he was still surprised.

Galenthern, the last dry and arid fringe of it at any rate, was far below. It was not the Galenthern that he knew though. It was brown rather than green. The swamps were dry forests with creeks, instead of the deep tracts of mud and mosquito-infested wetlands that he knew. But it was still Galenthern. And it was vast. And worst of all, home lay on its far side.

"I had no idea how high we'd come," he said.

"We're a long way up, all right," Erlissa answered.

She pointed with her staff. "See. That's the peak we want, or more accurately, we seek the tower under its shadow."

They were not only higher, but also much closer to their destination than Lanrik had reckoned. Before them was now a well-used mountain trail. It wound ahead between ridges, climbing ever higher. But people made such trails, and that made him wary, for wherever people traveled danger followed.

Everywhere he looked were shattered rocks. There were few trees, and those that he did see belonged to some stunted variety of pine that he did not know. He saw why the Halathrin had long ago named the range the Graèglin Dennath: the Ash Mountains. They usually named things truly. And yet this was one of the inhabited parts. It made him wonder about the rest of the land.

He had heard stories that the very air in this region could be poisonous, and that steam rose from cracks in the earth. The stories also mentioned lakes of boiling water. He would have to see *that* before he believed it. But on the other hand, he was going to keep an open mind on the subject.

"We'd better find a place to camp," he said. "And quickly. There's no chance of traveling through here during the day. There could be eyes on us from anywhere."

Erlissa looked around. "What about over there?"

Ahead was a clump of boulders and shattered rocks. It would offer shade from the hot sun, and best of all, it would also offer a hidden vantage point to watch for any sign of pursuing elugs, or anybody else that was around.

"Let's go," he said. "We probably won't find anywhere better."

They reached the boulders and dismounted. They led the horses by hand, and Lanrik drew his sword. He did

26

not know what was inside the tumbled rocks. There might be room for a dozen men.

His fears were needless. There was no one there. The air was cooler though, as he expected, for there were many small spots of shade. That would change during the day, but for a while at least the nighttime cool lingered and they would benefit by it.

They unsaddled the horses and fed them a ration of grain. Feed was always a problem, but in this land water was even scarcer. They would need to find a supply soon.

They ate a quick breakfast. It was only stale bread and dried strips of beef, but they did not feel like anything more. They had not quite finished when they heard a sound. It seemed at once dim and remote, and then loud and clear. It thrummed through the air for a long time, mostly deep and resonant, but sometimes wavery and sinuous, and then it ceased just as suddenly as it had started.

They looked at each other.

"I've heard that sound before," Erlissa said.

Lanrik had too. Beyond doubt, it was a talnak horn. He had winded one himself once, in what seemed another life. He remembered the strange instrument, gold mouthed and heavy, that he had taken from the shazrahad's tent. It told him one thing at least; the blower was an Azan, rather than an elug.

They waited. Lanrik was ready to slide up and onto a boulder to see what was happening, but just at that moment another horn answered. This one was much closer.

"That's from further down the valley," he said. "Probably from somewhere along the same path that we climbed during the night."

Erlissa looked at him, and her expression was troubled.

"Are we hunted already?"

4. Tall, Dark and Grim

Lanrik wanted to see what was happening. He stood on a pile of shattered rock and used it to help him clamber up one of the boulders. A moment later, Erlissa joined him.

They slid forward carefully, being sure to keep their heads down. A taller boulder to their left offered cover so that they could not be seen from higher up the trail. Most of the path, however, was visible from their vantage.

The road seemed deserted. Nor did they hear more horns, but they waited patiently. After some minutes, they saw a column of riders wind their way down the trail.

As expected, they were Azan. Lanrik counted fifty-three of them. The riders wore their customary robes, white and flowing, and colored headdresses. He noticed that none were the scarlet of a shazrahad.

They came close to the boulders. The noise of so many hooves over hard ground was loud, but the sweet jingle of small bells attached to the leather harnesses cut through it. No doubt such ornaments would be removed before combat.

Each man bore a tulwar in a hardened leather sheath at his side. The curved blades were ideal for use on horseback. Some also held spears, a less suitable weapon, but they were few and probably intended to be thrown at an enemy from a distance.

They carried no shields. Timber was scarce in this country, and defense did not suit their method of fighting anyway.

Exactly what these men were doing, he was not yet sure. One thing he did know: they were warriors. He could read that on them clearly, and he did not need to see their weapons to confirm it. The looks on their faces showed him more than enough. They were hard men, used to fighting and killing – or being killed.

They spoke little as they rode, but their voices were harsh when they did so. All the while they gazed about them carefully, but whether that was because they were searching for intruders, or due to habitual wariness, Lanrik could not be sure.

A few tense moments passed. He was ready to string his bow and shoot if the Azan saw the tracks left by him and Erlissa during the night, but the ground was hard, and if any trail was visible, it would likely be taken as alar marks.

The Azan apparently did not see anything unusual, for they kept riding. Their horses trotted nimbly down the steep trail, and the men only looked at the boulders with cursory interest.

When they had passed, Erlissa spoke. "I wonder if they're looking for us, or if something else is going on?"

"It's hard to know," Lanrik answered. "But this much is good – that was a lot of horses, and whatever tracks we made coming up here will now be harder to find or to follow."

She pursed her lips. "I suppose so. But I still wonder what those men were doing. They didn't really look like they were searching. But if not, why travel in such a large and well-armed group?"

"A good question," he said. "If I had to bet, I'd say that whatever they're doing doesn't concern us. But if that's right, it only makes me wonder all the more where they're going and what their purpose is."

They watched for a while longer to ensure that no one else came, or that the first group did not return. But there was no further sign of anybody, nor any other sounding of a talnak horn.

Lanrik put the Azan from his mind and concentrated on the task at hand. They would soon reach the dark tower that Erlissa had seen in her vision, and what then? What subterfuge could he attempt that would distract the elùgroths?

Nothing came to mind as the day wore on. The shade from the boulders lessened, and the air grew stifling hot. The sky, too bright to look at for long, was a washed out blue. Above, he saw eagles circle as they rode the air. From time to time he even heard their calls, high-pitched and shrill.

The eagles were not the only animals though. In the distance he heard the bleating of sheep. It was a familiar sound, even a reassuring one, but he reminded himself that wherever there was livestock there were also people.

They took turns to sleep while the day progressed. It was uncomfortable in the heat, but there was still some shade near the larger boulders, and that was useful.

Night fell swiftly when it came. The stars burned suddenly bright, almost as though someone had turned on a lamp, and though the air cooled quickly, the boulders, warmed by the sun all day, continued to radiate waves of heat.

They saddled their horses and mounted. Carefully, they made their way out of cover and rejoined the trail. If elugs followed them up the mountain, they need not be trackers to do so. There was only one main path, and they were on it. If the elugs stuck to that, they would likely find them.

For that reason, Lanrik knew that he and Erlissa must travel fast. And yet it was hard to travel at speed and still slip through an enemy country unnoticed.

They moved ahead up the trail. If anything, it grew steeper. Boulders and large outcrops of rock became common. To their left, the shoulder of the mountain hulked above them. Immediately to their right, a deep abyss fell away into a valley far below. What was down there, Lanrik could not guess. It was a sea of shadows, but whenever the horses dislodged a rock on the precipice, it tumbled down into the pit for a long time before the noise subsided.

It was a strange land, even more so at night. Enemies could be anywhere, or there could be nothing but endless ridges of rock and dust and dry air. Fumes and foul smells drifted on the ever-changing breeze. And yet, just now, he smelled once more the fragrance of cedar trees. It was a scent that he liked, and it reminded him that no matter how hostile this land seemed to him, it still held at least some beauty.

The narrow trail widened. In the dark he saw the shadowy outline of the trees themselves, and the sweet smell grew suddenly strong. It was not a forest; there seemed no chance of such a thing in the Graèglin Dennath, and yet it was as close to it as was possible in this land of shattered stone and arid soil.

"The road grows level," Erlissa whispered in the dark.

They slowed down. They were on a high plateau of some kind. Dimly, he saw that there was grass here. More than he had seen in many days. No doubt it was brown and stunted, but it was still *grass*.

A little further ahead he saw the source of the bleating sheep. A pen stood there, built of piled rock, perhaps a quarter of an acre in size. The sheep huddled inside it, gated in by a makeshift panel of small branches and rope that fenced off a gap in the rocks. It was a flimsy thing, but it worked.

They came to a second pen. This was smaller and there were half a dozen horses in it. The rock walls were piled higher, and here was a proper gate. The horses inside came over and stuck their heads over its top to investigate.

Lanrik's mount twitched its ears, and he looked at the new horses himself. As with all the alar that he had ever seen, these were fine animals. After a moment, one came closer and Lanrik watched it.

Even in the dark he could see that it was a roan. It was a color that he had never noticed with an alar horse before. He stopped, and Erlissa waited for him. A good while he studied the horse, sure that he knew it. It stretched out its neck toward him and snorted softly.

Erlissa leaned in her saddle toward him.

"What is it?" she asked.

The horse was further away from her and harder to see. But her lack of recognition did not alter his own certainty.

"It's Aranloth's roan," he said.

Erlissa leaned even closer. "We're very near then. But that, we already knew. Shall we take it?"

He grinned at her in the dark "Who's the horse thief now?"

She laughed softly. It was a faint and hushed sound in the dark, but it was good to hear.

"I've been spending too much time with you. Your habits are rubbing off on me."

"Maybe some of the good ones too, I hope."

"Anything is possible."

Lanrik looked back at the horse. He wanted to take it, but it was not wise.

"Better to wait until we make our way back," he said. If circumstances allow, we'll get it then. If we do so now, it'll only stir up the Azan. They'll start looking for whoever took it."

They nudged their horses forward. He had no great confidence that they would be coming back, and even if they did, they would likely not have the chance or time to stop for the roan, but he made a promise to himself to try.

Something else was also on his mind. Where stock were kept, people were close to hand. But not only that, there must also be water.

He loosened the reins and let his mount choose its own way forward. If there was water, the horse would smell it, and being thirsty, would head toward it. At least, so he hoped.

They moved ahead slowly. Even so, the horses made noise, but it was not much. Ahead was a group of huts. Light spilled out from some, and he heard voices. They were right in the midst of their enemies. Yet no alarm was raised and they continued forward in the dark.

Lanrik smelled smoke from various fires. It was not from burning timber, but rather from dry animal dung. The aroma of cooked food also lingered in the air. They drew level with the huts. His heart raced. Erlissa, as ever, seemed to ride calmly beside him, and after a few moments they were through.

The village was behind them, soon lost in the dark except for the lights from inside. Moments later, they discovered water. He need not have bothered letting the horses find it. It was right by the side of the road.

A high ridge of steep rock and stone bulked above them in the night. Beneath that, and just to the left side of the road, were a series of rock pools. They narrow and shallow, but presumably filled by some sort of spring that found its source in the slope above and gathered in the basins.

The basins, he suspected, were formed by hand rather than natural. The Azan had made them to collect the water and to prevent it seeping back into the earth.

The horses trotted toward them. Their hooves clicked over the stones, but the huts were far enough back that the noise should not be heard.

Lanrik let his mount drink, but he nocked an arrow to his bow and watched. Erlissa dismounted and filled her water bag. When she was done, she kneeled and drank herself. Then she took his water bag and filled it also. All the while he kept an eye out for the enemy. Water was rare in this land, so precious that the Azan might guard it.

He saw nothing. When the horses had taken their fill, and Erlissa remounted, he drank a little from his refilled water bag. The taste was as foreign to him as everything else in this land. He detected many minerals, including salt, but it was the hint of sulfur that stood out most. Even in trace amounts it was unpleasant, but that did not mean the water was unhealthy. Evidently, the sheep and horses, and no doubt the Azan in the huts drank it.

He made to move back along the road, but Erlissa shook her head.

"This way," she whispered.

She nudged her mount forward, and it picked its way between several basins, coming out onto a smooth shelf of rock that funneled the water into them. The rock here was slick, and Lanrik's horse struggled with its footing. But he followed her and after a moment the shelf broke up into shattered stone and then, unexpectedly, there was another path.

That it was seldom used, he saw straight away. And it was steep too. How Erlissa had found it, he did not know. He expected that she knew it from her vision, rather than that she had seen it while they drank.

At any rate, she showed no doubt about this new trail. She led the way with confidence. He had a feeling that the previous road skirted the ridges and valleys, providing a good way through into neighboring lands and villages. This new path, steep and rarely trodden, probably only led to one place: the dark tower beneath the mountain peak. They were close now. Not only to Aranloth, but also to the elùgroths who held him captive.

Lanrik turned the situation over in his mind. They still had no plan, and it worried him. He did not like the feeling at all, for usually he could think of *something*. Yet perhaps ideas would come to mind when he saw the tower with his own eyes.

They followed the winding path. It was so steep that Lanrik felt dizzy thinking of the long slide down behind him and the vast gulf of air that opened up in turns to left or right, depending on the twists of the road. Should the horses misstep, or should enemies attack, they were dead.

He concentrated on the narrow trail ahead. Erlissa stayed in the front. She knew that he was not good with heights. Just as well that it was dark. It would be worse if he could see the land dropping away to the sides.

There seemed no end to their climbing. They were now high up the mountain, and the towering peak must overshadow them, if only there was light enough to see it by. But he felt it there nevertheless, and saw something of its dim outline.

There was enough light to see something else. This was much closer. It was on the ground just before him, an impression in a run of sand that crossed the road: a drùgluck sign. The elug's mark to be wary of danger, or sorcery, or both. Only this was not made by an elug. It came from the heel of a boot, and only elùgroths did that. It was a warning not to follow them.

The mountain breeze blew suddenly colder and cut right though him.

"Elùgroths have trod this path," he said.

"I know," Erlissa replied. "But they're not on the path now. They're all at the tower."

Lanrik wished he could be so sure, but he did not voice his doubt. At least one thing was certain; Erlissa had learned some tracking skills from him, or at least the habit of studying the ground as they rode. There was a time that she would have been oblivious to such things.

They kept going. Road or no road, drùgluck signs or not, Erlissa knew where she was headed. She needed nothing save her seeker sense to confirm that she was on the right path.

But they saw further evidence anyway. From above, a sudden light flared, white and dazzling. The ragged mountain peak was lit by it. Stone towered above them. The summit was near, jutting out overhead like an outthrust jaw. Below it, the light blazed brighter. They saw the shape of a tower, tall, dark and grim. With a final flare the light flickered out and the world fell into dark again. The night now seemed doubly black, and then a slow boom lurched over the stony slopes toward them. Dust rose in the air. Small rocks fell from the sides of the road and clattered down the steep banks. The horses grew skittish.

"That was the sorcerer's citadel," Erlissa said. "Aranloth still holds off the enemy. He yet lives."

They continued without another word. The lòhren was alive, that much was clear. It would take more than a few elùgroths to kill him. Then again, there were more than a few surrounding him, otherwise he would not be trapped.

The tracks of elùgroths were all about them now. The road, wherever sand covered it, showed them by the dozen. It had the desired effect, for the three slanting lines, formed by iron bars fixed to their heels, sent a shiver running up his spine.

And now it was not only on the road. The sign was carved into the very rock of the cliff when they turned a corner. Some sort of ocher half-filled the deep grooves. It gleamed eerily in the dark, and no stronger warning could be given to stay away from this place.

Lanrik did not doubt that neither elugs nor Azan ever came this way. This was a forbidden place. It had been so for a long time. The carving on the rock was old and weathered, made smooth in part by wind and blowing sand, but mostly by rain. And in these mountains, that would take centuries.

The horses trudged onward into the night. The stars glinted in the great dark above. Lanrik noticed Halathgar, the constellation of the Lost Huntress. It at least was the same here as it was at home, if nothing else in this strange land was familiar to him.

At length, dawn came. So too the end of their long journey. The sun was a crimson ball that rose, slowly but surely, above the rim of the mountains. Peak after peak kindled red, as though they were formed of iron and heated in a furnace. Light danced like fire, running from ridge to ridge, from rock face to rock face, and the dark sky eased from black to blue. It would not last long. Soon the heat would begin, and the blue would transform into a blasting white-gold haze, full of harsh light that drained color.

Perhaps a quarter of a mile below them, on a slope of the mountain and still in the morning shadow of the peak, Lanrik saw the tower.

"You described it well," he said.

"Yes," she answered.

"Even I can sense the evil that lurks there, or at least was once the lifeblood of the land."

Erlissa nodded. "It reeks of Assurah."

He gave the tower a final glance. "We'd better get under cover. The light grows by the second and there are elùgroths there."

They moved off the track and dismounted behind a group of boulders. He was not overly worried about someone coming up behind them on the trail. He doubted it was used by anybody save elùgroths, and they were already down below.

They left the horses and crawled out to the side of the boulders, looking down across the slope toward the tower. The road traversed the higher parts of a ridge, and then dropped down at a steep angle to run to the tower's base. Elsewhere, the slope was covered in broken rocks.

The tower stood alone. There were no other buildings, or trees, or even any bushes. There was nothing but the column of dark stone and the black-clad elùgroths below it.

The sorcerers, probably a dozen of them, gathered not far from its base. Some stood. Others sat in a wedge, facing the tower. Their wych-wood staffs all pointed toward the tower's base. No doubt they continued to work their elùgai. Of Aranloth, there was no sign, yet Lanrik knew he was there.

"I feel him," Erlissa said.

Lanrik did not reply. A sense of hopelessness settled over him. He had known there would be elùgroths. He had known they could not challenge them directly. But as he looked at the tower and the bare rock and ground that surrounded it, he knew it was impossible to get to their friend unseen.

"We cannot reach him," he said. "The whole place is better guarded than Seven Devil Peak."

Erlissa turned to him. Her face was grim. "The way is blocked to us." She hesitated. "Yet I saw something else in my vision. I did not speak of it for fear. Now, I know that there is no other chance."

5. The Roots of the Mountain

Lanrik saw lines of worry and doubt on Erlissa's face. Whatever this other way was, he would like it no more than she. Yet Aranloth needed help, and so he knew before she said any more that he would undertake the risk, no matter what.

"Tell me of this other choice," he said.

Erlissa held her staff close. She closed her eyes and spoke, though whence her knowledge came he could not tell. It seemed in part something that she had learned as a lòhren, in part something that she had intuited during her vision.

"This is an ancient land," she began. "Once, it was home to Assurah. It was far more populous then. But now, few villages remain, and no elùgroths dwell here."

Lanrik pointed to the tower. "There are plenty enough down there."

"Yes, but they aren't from here. The tower is abandoned. Those elùgroths tracked Aranloth as he wandered the Graèglin Dennath. I think they set upon him here by surprise. They do not know this land."

"Neither do we," Lanrik said.

"No. Not you. Not them. Not Aranloth. But I'm a seeker. I find things, and my vision of Aranloth showed me a way. But you will not like it…"

"Tell me anyway," he answered.

She opened her eyes. "The tower is built upon a foundation of rock. Ùhrengai supports and infuses it, as is common with such places – even Lòrenta. Before the tower was built, it was long a place of worship and sorcery. Aranloth would have sensed as much. But he would not know what lies beneath. I, however, saw that with my seeker vision. There are pits, tunnels and caves. Some are natural, some formed by hand from a time before Alithoras knew either lòhrens or Halathrin."

She hesitated, looking down at the tower grimly before she started again.

"It was once a place of human sacrifice. Some paths beneath the earth lead to fire and death. Some to never-ending blackness. One way, and one alone, leads to the base of the tower. Assurah knew it. Right below the tower's foundations lies a great pit: unexplored and shunned long ago by the villagers of this land. But it provides a way in for us, and a way out for Aranloth."

"If there's known to be a pit there, why haven't the elùgroths gone in that way to attack Aranloth?"

"They know the pit is there. They also know that something lives within it, some dark remnant of Assurah's sorcery. But they do not know that a passage connects it to the outside world."

"What of this thing that lives in the pit? Tell me more about it."

"I'm not sure what it is. Something evil, that much I sense. And it is not alone."

"And there's no other way in?"

"No. There is not."

Lanrik thought about this new information. Erlissa was right. He did not like it. But he had no other plan, and no prospect of thinking of one. The way forward was clear.

"Then we'll just have to attempt it. There's nothing else to try."

Erlissa looked at him gravely and did not answer.

They waited through a long day. It was hot once more, and toward its end they gave the horses much of the precious water that they carried.

The sun set. It grew cold more swiftly than Lanrik would have believed before he had come to this land.

Below, a strange noise rose. It was an eerie chanting, full of harsh sounds and repeated words. It rolled over shattered rocks, echoing and re-echoing without beginning or end, and even the craggy peak of the mountain leaning over the valley seemed to whisper it back.

Erlissa stirred. "The elùgroths work a new kind of sorcery."

White light flared from the tower top, and the chanting grew erratic and lost momentum.

"Aranloth answers them," Lanrik said.

They listened in the dark a while longer. The chanting ceased, and no further light sprang to life. Lanrik wondered how Aranloth, alone and unaided, had held off so many attackers for so long. That the lòhren was powerful, he knew. Though so too was Elù-Randùr. Which of them was more mighty, he did not know. But Elù-Randùr at least had help, even if the other elùgroths had not reached his mastery.

"It's time to go," Erlissa said. "This will be a long night, and a longer day will follow on its heels."

They remounted. Without another word, Erlissa led the way from their camp, such as it had been.

She did not speak. Her head was bowed, and she gripped her walnut staff tightly in her hand. It seemed to Lanrik that she rode in some sort of trance. It was not as deep as the last one, perhaps merely a sending out of her lòhren senses. Whatever she did, she did it in silence, and he left her to concentrate.

43

They backtracked along the road that they had climbed last night, but they did not go far. Within several hundred paces Erlissa pulled up her mount.

She sat astride it a while, still and thoughtful. The horse grew restless under her, stepping a little to the side, but she ignored it.

After some moments, she nudged her mount toward the edge of the road. There were bushes here, or perhaps small trees; Lanrik could not tell in the dark. What he did learn swiftly was that they were thorny.

Erlissa encouraged her horse forward, for there was a way between the crowding branches, though it was narrow. Many times the long thorns pricked and gashed them.

It was a large thicket. When they finally reached the other side all that stood before them was a rugged rock face.

A while they stared at it. Erlissa was no longer in a trance and now looked about alertly. Lanrik spoke.

"This doesn't look promising."

"No," she answered. "And yet the entrance is here, or at least nearby. I know it."

Lanrik dismounted. He tied his mount's reins around a thorny branch and moved a little to the right. He saw nothing. There was no change in the rock face. He pushed as deep as he dared into a stand of the thorny trees. He had nearly turned to go back when he noticed something.

There was a path on the ground, disappearing into the thicket and toward the road. Obviously, it was an animal trail of some kind, and though it was wide, he saw no paw or hoof tracks. That was unusual, though perhaps something was in fact there but it was too dark to see it. What interested him was that animal trails always led from one place to another. And yet, such a large animal as this obviously could not clamber down the steep rock face. But that was where the trail started.

He stepped closer and studied the craggy surface. Sure enough, there was a fissure in the rock, obscured by a slight bulge in the cliff face that made it appear no more than a shadow.

The fissure was not quite man high, and only wide enough for someone to squeeze through sideways, but it was an opening nonetheless.

"I've found it," he called.

Erlissa tied her own reins tightly around a branch and joined him. They stood a while before the crack. They knew that they must pass through it, but they were not keen to do so.

To either side of it, so faint as to be barely visible, were drùgluck signs. Time and nature had weathered them so badly as to render the rough chisel strokes near invisible.

No doubt this cave, for such it must be, was long forgotten. There was no sign that people had ever come here save for the ancient marks. They served as a warning to superstitious elugs, and probably Azan also, that this place must be shunned, unless, perhaps, in the presence of an elùgroth conducting some rite or ceremony.

The drùgluck signs were not the only worry. Whatever made the track led from the fissure, and it was a large animal of some sort. Lanrik did not know what it was, nor did he want to find out. How it even forced a way though such a narrow crevice, he did not know. He saw no fur or hair caught on the sides. But something lived in there, making its home amid the dark at the roots of the mountain.

There was an odor also. It was not the smell of an animal lair. It was something else. Legends told of poisoned air in these lands, of crannies in the rock that expelled noxious gases. But he took heart. Those stories told of air that killed without scent. If he could smell it, and he did, it was not such a place. And the creature, whatever it was, lived and breathed somewhere inside.

"We can't stand here all night," Erlissa said.

She took a good grip of her staff and stepped forward. Light flickered at its tip. Taking her time, she tilted it into the cave and peered inside. Evidently she saw nothing that disturbed her, for a moment later she squeezed through the crack.

Lanrik now stood alone in the dark. He did not wish to leave the horses; they were escape and life in this vast land of enemies. But they were securely tethered and would not wander off. They were also far enough away from the road that no one should find them, even if someone came this way.

It worried him that should he and Erlissa never return no one would untie them. Although if that was the case, eventually thirst would likely drive them to break free and make their way back to the water in the Azan village.

After a final glance at them, he slipped through the crack and joined Erlissa. What they would find, he did not know. Whether they would actually free Aranloth, he could not guess. But one thing about this night was certain: nothing was going to be easy.

6. A Sea of Death

It was warmer in the cave. The light from Erlissa's staff cast strange shadows over the nearby walls and ceiling. They stepped forward cautiously along a narrow and rough passage.

Debris covered the floor. Lanrik trod carefully, picking a path through sand, scattered rock and what he took to be bones.

He squatted down and examined the latter. That some were human, he did not doubt, though how they had come to be here he could not be sure. But many were gnawed and splintered, the tooth marks of a large animal obvious even in the dim light.

He stood up. Something had lived in here. Or some group of things. But these bones were old. They had lain in the cave for decades, or even hundreds of years, although whatever made the path from the rock face into the thicket lived here *now*. Such a path would not survive beyond a few years if not refreshed by frequent use.

Erlissa continued, walking slowly but with confidence, and he followed. Soon the cave widened. The floor smoothed out, and the bones and other debris disappeared. What stood out now were smoke stains on the ceiling. He saw the remnants of fire-pits in the middle of the floor. Flames had lit this chamber, long and often.

Soot was not the only thing that stood out. The light from Erlissa's staff flared a little brighter and revealed wall paintings. They covered the dull stone with bright images in yellow and red ochre. Many were of strange creatures: beasts, birds and trees shaped like none that he had ever seen or imagined. Whether they were real or legendary he did not know. It was a strange land, and he was not swift to classify the unknown as impossible just because he had never seen it in the flesh.

Other things he recognized. There were images of elùgroths with their wych-wood staffs, massive lethrin and bow-legged elugs. But mostly, he saw the desert-dwelling animals of these high mountains.

"They look fresh enough that they could have been painted yesterday," he said.

"So they do," Erlissa answered. "But they're as old as the drùgluck sign outside – or older."

They paused a little, looking about them in wonder at so much detail and so much accuracy in the seemingly simple paintings. But they did not linger long. Soon, they moved ahead.

The cave narrowed again. For a good way they walked in the near dark. The floor slanted downward, but the angle was not steep. After several minutes, Erlissa's shuffling feet came to a stop.

Before them the tunnel forked. One path, veering a little to the left, continued at the same slope. The other, turning somewhat to the right, plummeted steeply. It gaped like a dark pit before them.

"Which way?" he asked.

Erlissa hesitated. Her head swiveled from side to side, but her eyes were closed. What senses she used, he did not know, but they were different from the ones that he relied upon.

The steep tunnel frightened him, though he did not know why. A faint smell of bad air drifted from the other.

"We'll take the steep one," Erlissa said. There was no doubt in her voice.

She led the way forward again. The angle was significant, but the floor was smooth and hard, without loose rock or sand. They made good time. There was no sign of life here; no paintings or fires or dried grasses blown in from outside. There was nothing but a tunnel that drove into the dark heart of the mountain like a stake. It was a way that even the ancients who knew this place might have feared to tread.

They went on. They were deep underground now, and the weight of measureless stone piled above. The floor turned to sand. It was loose under their boots, and deep. Lanrik bent down and ran a hand through it. It gleamed white beneath Erlissa's light. It was pure, without soil or silt, and the grains were large and sharp edged. He let it slip through his fingers and continued.

Unexpectedly, the floor levelled out. How deep they were, he could not tell. Perhaps they had descended to the level of the black tower. Maybe they had gone deeper.

Water bubbled from a crack in the wall to their right. It was a spring, fed, he supposed, from the mountain slopes somewhere above. It ran in a narrow channel across the passage.

They paused, and he bent down to dip his fingers into it. He took them out again quickly and stood.

"It's *hot*," he said.

Erlissa nodded. "It comes from deep in the earth. Deeper than any tunnel carved or found by man."

They stepped over the channel and moved ahead. The ground remained level, and the way widened further. For the first time, he heard noise, though he could not identify it. It was a dull squeaking. And the air began to smell. Swiftly, the odor grew strong until it was a sharp stench.

The noise became louder. Erlissa wrinkled her nose in distaste.

"Bats," she said.

He smiled in the dark. The smell was obnoxious, but it reassured him that there was life down here. If the bats could survive, so too could he and Erlissa, even if she was not best pleased with the surroundings.

They moved ahead into a larger cavern. Bats clung to the ragged rock faces. Thousands of them. They did not like the light, and grew agitated. Erlissa dimmed it, till it was just enough to see by, and they made their way through the chamber.

The smell was nauseating. They trod carefully, for the floor was deep in droppings. There were dead bats too. And here at least, if he had not seen any elsewhere in the cave, were insects; living, feeding, scurrying within the piles of bat dung and turning it over.

Erlissa retched, but she made no move to get through the cavern faster. Wary of danger, she stepped at the same pace, seeking the way forward as carefully as ever.

Eventually, the chamber narrowed once more and the bats grew less numerous, until at last they were gone. But the stench remained, if not quite as strong. The tunnel dropped down even more steeply at this point.

The smell petered out rapidly now, for the cavern had been warmed by the bodies of so many bats, and the warm air rose, carrying much of the odor with it.

Erlissa paused. A sheen of sweat gleamed on her face, and her skin looked sickly.

"That was revolting," she whispered.

"Yes, but I noticed this at least. There were no tracks in that cave. We should be alone down here, for nothing could fail to leave a trail on the floor in there."

"Well, I'm glad *you* found some use for all that muck."

He smiled. "A Raithlin never lets slip an opportunity."

She gave him a look of disgust and moved on.

Once again the tunnel levelled out. It widened too, swiftly this time, and they were now in an open space. This was a vast cavern, but the ceiling was low, barely above their heads. The floor was of solid rock, slick with moisture. They went ahead, now walking side by side.

The rock grew wetter, and beaded moisture dripped from the walls. It was suddenly warm too.

"I don't like this place," Erlissa said.

Lanrik had learned to trust her instincts. He was unsure of whether to nock an arrow or draw his sword. He chose the sword, and it felt good in his hand. *Conhain's sword.* It still gave him a thrill to touch it, more so to think that he had spoken with the great man himself, or at least his spirit. That he was descended from him was a shock. He had achieved some measure of his own success, served his country well, but he was not Conhain and could never match his deeds. Yet it was good to know that some remnant of the great man's blood ran through his own veins.

Erlissa paused, and Lanrik realized his mind was wandering. He could not afford that. He looked ahead and saw why she had come to a stop.

There was a dip in the cavern, and a body of water lay ahead of them. The light of Erlissa's staff flared brighter, and it shone out, racing ahead.

The light revealed a lake, but like none that Lanrik had ever seen. The water was evidently hot, for steam rose up from it in wispy clouds, and moisture, condensing on the roof close above, dripped down ceaselessly to disturb the otherwise still surface.

There was no way forward save for a path on the right. The ground rose highest there, but the way was narrow and close to the lake.

"Don't touch the water," Erlissa said.

Lanrik wondered if that warning was because it was hot, or for some other reason, but she did not explain. Instead, she moved to the right and struck out across the narrow path. She did not reduce the light, and even as they walked ahead, he still saw no sign of the far shore.

They walked cautiously. It was difficult to keep a good footing on the slick rock, but they hugged the wall where the ground was marginally drier.

Peering ahead through the vaporous air, Lanrik now saw to the other side of the lake. It was not that distant. A moment later, he noticed a ripple in the water far out to the left. What it was, he did not know, but it seemed larger than the disturbances caused by the dripping from above, and the shore suddenly seemed much further away.

They kept going, and he fixed his gaze out over the water, a sense of danger prickling his skin. He saw no more movement though.

The shore loomed closer now, but the land bridge over which they trod narrowed. It tilted at a steeper angle as well, sloping down toward the water. Erlissa slowed, and Lanrik kept scanning the water.

There was movement again. This time much closer. The water was deeper than he had guessed, for something large swam within it, and yet for all its size it stayed below the surface. All he saw was a growing wave of water that rose up, frothing and steaming at its crest.

"Hurry!" he said. "Something's in the water!"

Erlissa did not move. She stood a moment, looking out over the lake, a determined expression on her face.

"Running is no good," she answered.

Lanrik did not know what she meant. The way ahead was clear, but he trusted her. He too stood his ground. He put his back to the wall and kept a firm grip on Conhain's sword.

Whatever swam in the water gathered speed. It struck out toward them now swiftly. The wave rose higher, perhaps to knee level.

Too late Lanrik realized what Erlissa already knew. The creature would not attack directly. Instead, it used the wave. The simmering water would roll over the little land bridge, and then smash into the wall behind them before draining back into the lake in a great rush. The mass of water would surely sweep them with it as it returned. In the lake, they would be at the creature's mercy, and neither sword nor bow would be any help to him.

He pressed back against the wall, and squatted down, bracing himself against it. Erlissa, however, remained where she was. At the last second several things happened at once.

Whatever creature this was, it turned and thrashed, propelling the wave with a final lash of power. He caught a glimpse of it then, large and sinuous, finned, but not a fish. It threw up great loops of its body, three of them rising high above the surface of the water, scaled and moss-slicked. Its back was gray and dull, but its belly was pearlescent.

The wave smashed into the land bridge, cascading toward them. At the last moment, light flared from Erlissa's staff.

Blue lòhren-fire lit the vast cavern, but she did not attack the creature. Instead, the fire formed a shield. The water pounded against it. A hiss filled the cavern, and a cloud of steam billowed out to hang over the lake. After a few seconds both light and wave disappeared.

"Run!" Erlissa cried.

She had given them a chance, and they took it. With a final glance at the water, Lanrik sprinted. He saw nothing through all the steam, but the creature was there, and close, for he heard it in the water nearby.

They raced ahead, wary of the slick stone beneath their boots, but risking it. The land bridge widened quickly. The creature was not just large, but intelligent. It had timed its attack for the moment of greatest vulnerability.

They sped forward. Several times they nearly fell, but managed to scramble to the other side of the lake. The great body of water lay behind them now, a seething, rippling, churning mass that lapped angrily at its banks like a live thing trying to clamber out of a declivity that held it captive.

Lanrik backed away, running his gaze all over the surface for any sign of the creature, but it did not follow them. It must have slipped into deeper water, there to mull over its failure and plan better for its next attack.

"What *was* that," he said.

Erlissa did not waver in her scrutiny of the water.

"I don't know. I've never heard of its like before, but I think it's descended from creatures bred in Assurah's time. Much evil was done in this place, and this was not the greatest."

They kept backing away until the lake dwindled from sight. Even then, they could not be sure if the creature was capable of following them. There was no way to know, for they had seen so little of it that they could not tell if it was confined to water or if it could walk, crawl or writhe over land. Still less did they know how persistent it was as a hunter.

The tunnel about them closed in once more, and they now hurried ahead listening for any sign of pursuit. The floor began to rise, and they moved upward toward the tower. Somewhere, it was built above them.

Now, many side tunnels issued from the main one. Where they led, Lanrik did not know, nor did he ask. If Erlissa knew, she said nothing. Instead, she led him onward with complete confidence. If her pace slowed, it was not because she did not know the way, but that she feared what they would find when they reached their destination.

After some while Lanrik felt a throbbing sensation travel up through the earth. It was faint at first, a rumbling tremor that tickled his boots or that he felt with his fingers if he ran a hand along the wall. From time to time, fine dust coming down from the roof drifted through the air

"The elùgroths are near," she said. "They work their sorcery, trying to topple the tower, but Aranloth resists them still."

"Just as well," he answered. "Should the tower fall, these caverns would likely collapse beneath it."

"Then we'd better hasten, for he cannot fight them off forever. He falters, that much I can tell even from here."

Despite her words she did not hurry any more than she already had been, and the light from her staff died down to the faintest flicker as though she sought to hide their presence from anything else that dwelled down here.

He did not possess the lòhren-senses that she used, but he relied on his own natural ones. Sight was limited; hearing told him little. Smell worried him – there was a growing odor of decay in the air. Instinct also came to the fore, whatever combination of his senses and his experience that it entailed. He knew that great danger lay ahead, and not just from the elùgroths. He felt it all around; a presence of evil that seeped through the surrounding rock like water through sand.

The tunnel they followed turned a corner. The air opened up around them. They now stood in a cavern again. The whispering echo of their quiet footsteps told him that it was large. The wall remained on their left, close enough that they could still touch it. But to the right was empty space. How much, he did not know until Erlissa raised her staff and its light flickered more brightly.

The sudden radiance flashed and flared. It swelled, striking out against the dark and sending it skittering back hundreds of paces to the far wall.

It was not so much a cavern, as a vast pit. They stood upon its rim, the tunnel they were in transforming into a narrow ledge carved into the wall and climbing toward an iron door, massive and rusted, at the top. The door was round, shaped to represent a drùgluck sign, with three iron struts crossing it sideways.

Lanrik took a step ahead, but Erlissa put a hand on his shoulder.

"It's here," she said.

"What is?"

"That which guards this place. The evil that has lived here since Assurah's time."

He paused. The pit was not empty.

Erlissa pointed the staff downward, and what its light revealed appalled him. The pit was filled with bones; the long bones of human legs and arms. Rib bones. Small bones and hollow-socketed skulls. They all lay together in a mass, deep as a lake.

And then, white and tumbling, as though they were part of a churning sea of human death, the bones seethed. A noise came to his ears at the same time. It was no crashing of waves, no lapping of water against a bank. It was a dry and dusty rattle.

Something moved far down within the pit of death, and it swam through the loose bones toward the surface.

7. The Last Swamp

Talgin waited patiently for a report.

He saw that the scouts were returning now, but he already knew what they would say when they reached him. Did nothing ever go according to plan?

He watched as the Raithlin rode toward him over the plain. The grass was dry and stunted, and there was a risk of the horses kicking up a dust cloud behind them. That would mark their location to the enemy, if the enemy did not already know it. But they *did* know it. Of that, he was sure.

The Raithlin knew what they were doing though. They traveled with speed, which was not a good sign, but they held the pace back enough so that they raised little dust. Also, they stayed away from each other in order to ensure that what dust there was could not come together and form a prominent cloud.

They neared the fringe of trees under which he stood. He, and the remaining eighteen Raithlin. The returning riders made twenty-one: all that was left of the original hundred.

It could be worse, he supposed. But it could be better too. He would never forgive the king for disbanding the Raithlin, and then allowing Ebona into the city. Nor would he forgive the Witch-queen. The blood of scores of Raithlin was on her hands, and he would make her pay for that. At least, if he lived long enough.

Revenge, he contemplated, was better suited to the young – they had the time to accomplish it. He was beginning to feel old, far too old to think that he would see the final outcome of the struggle now playing out.

Arawdan approached, riding from the bright sun of the plains into the dark shade beneath the fringe of trees. He pulled up his mount. The other two came in at the same time, but Arawdan spoke first, being the most senior.

"They come, Lindrath. The enemy has our trail. We have no more than an hour before they reach this place."

Talgin did not like being called Lindrath anymore. The title was no longer his, but the men did not know that. Not yet, anyway.

"How many?"

Arawdan answered without hesitation. "A troop of one hundred."

Talgin did not need to ask him if he was sure. He was a Raithlin, and they did not make mistakes about such matters. It was a lot of Royal Guards, but perhaps he should be grateful it was not a thousand.

He glanced around him at the men. They were badly outnumbered and they must avoid their pursuers, at least until they found a way to turn things to their advantage. Avoiding them was no problem in itself, or it would not be if that was their only concern. But they had a reason not to stray far from where they were. They waited, on the southern edge of Galenthern, on the rim of the last swamp, for Lanrik and Erlissa's return. Hopefully, with the lòhren Aranloth.

He signaled the men with a wave of his hand.

"We go into the swamp," he said. "Stay on the main trail."

They formed a column and passed through the fringe of trees. As they rode, other Raithlin joined them, until all twenty-one were in the line.

He hoped the guards would not follow them. That they could was obvious. They had passable trackers with them, and by necessity the trail left by his men, a large group on horseback, was near impossible to hide.

The guards had no doubt ventured into Galenthern to find them. The trail from the tor to here being plain, they had pursued. Whether they would risk entering the swamp was another matter. But Ebona was their mistress, and to return to her and report failure was not something that they would like to do. It was a pity, but the guards would come after them, even if the advantage of their numbers was diminished in an environment better suited to the Raithlin.

One of the men behind him spoke.

"Lindrath. Should we try to hide our trail?"

Talgin shook his head. "It would take too long. If they follow us, they follow us. Let's just hope, for all our sakes, that they don't."

Ebona would have given her guards instructions. They were probably warned of the consequences of returning without first destroying what was left of the Raithlin. His own escape, as well as that of Lanrik and Erlissa from Esgallien, had embarrassed her and weakened her authority. The best way for her to redress that was to destroy the Raithlin, and then to bring back irrefutable evidence of it. Especially if that proof included the bodies of himself, Lanrik and Erlissa. The three of them had made a fool of her, and she would neither like nor forget it.

He remembered the look on her face outside the park in Esgallien. She seemed scared then, as she had a right to be. Conhain's ghost had an effect on everyone, but to her it must have been like her past catching up with her; a past that she had thought forgotten and buried.

One thing that was not a ghost was Conhain's sword, held in Lanrik's flesh and blood grip. She had seen *that* too. He was certain, for it was not the sort of thing that anyone could miss. It was a mighty sword, a Halathrin blade, and she would recognize it because of that even if she had not seen it with her own eyes in the days of old.

He wondered if Ebona knew through her witchery that Lanrik was descended from Conhain. Maybe she did, but if not, she would guess it. The great swords of the ancient Camar chieftains were only passed down to direct descendants. And no sword was ever more precious than the one the Halathrin gave to Conhain. Why his son did not inherit it, he did not know, and what it was called, for all such swords had names, he could not recall. That was another worrisome sign of age.

The column wound its way deeper into the swamp, and after an hour of slow riding he called a halt. It would let horses and men rest, and give the one Raithlin he had left behind a chance to catch up and report on whether or not their opponents had chosen to enter the swamp.

They remained quiet. There was food, though provisions were scarce, and it consisted mainly of dried game meat. They were lucky to have come across a herd of aurochs not long before Lanrik and Erlissa left them. Their meat was always satisfactory, and on this occasion he had sent three men to stalk them. The result was unexpectedly good: three kills and food to last them for a while, if they eked it out with tubers and berries.

His gaze swept over the surroundings. It was not really like the swamps that he was familiar with. There was little water for one thing. And the trees were taller and sparser. He recognized many plants, but many were different too, though some of these looked safe to eat.

They dare not try them though, unless hunger drove them to it later.

Everything depended on when, or if, Lanrik and Erlissa returned. He promised them that the Raithlin would remain in this swamp as long as they could. And if not at its fringe, somewhere along the main trail through its center. He had offered to take all the Raithlin to the Graèglin Dennath with them, but Lanrik decided against it. Stealth and secrecy was their only chance to free Aranloth. Too many horses and too many people would be seen, followed and set upon. Lanrik was right, but waiting without knowledge of what was going on to the south was hard.

He looked back down the path that they had traveled. There was no sign of the last scout that he had sent to observe the Royal Guards. That could mean good news – the guards had not followed them. Or it might mean he was captured. Either way, he could delay no longer. It was time to move again.

"Let's ride," he said.

The men mounted and got ready, but before they started out the scout came into view and hurried along the trail. He rode straight to Talgin.

"They've entered the swamp," the man said.

Talgin sighed. "All of them?"

"Yes, Lindrath."

"They mean to force a fight," he said. He shook his head at their thirst for blood.

"They ride warily though. They know the swamp favors us."

"So it does, but that doesn't change the fact that it's three to one, and they know it. Confidence outstrips their wariness."

The man sat silent on his steed. He had nothing further to report.

Talgin searched the column and signaled for the brothers Arawdan and Arawnus to come over.

He turned back to the scout. "Spread the news among the men."

The scout moved off and the two brothers approached and pulled up their horses.

"The guards follow us," he said.

The brothers showed no surprise.

"Shall we leave the swamp and lead them on a game of cat and mouse?" Arawnus asked.

"We could," Talgin said. "But that would only be putting things off. Sooner or later they would catch up with us and force the issue, whether it was on the plains or in this swamp. And we can't afford to miss Lanrik and Erlissa when they return. If they do. When that happens they'll likely need our help, and they'll probably need it quickly."

"Then there's nothing else for it," Arawdan said.

Talgin gave a slight nod. These were the two best Raithlin apart from Lanrik, and they understood what was needed.

"Go ahead and find a suitable place," he said.

They required no further explanation. After exchanging a quick glance among themselves, they turned their horses and trotted off.

Talgin signaled the column to move forward. The two brothers traveled ahead at a faster pace, but the line of Raithlin would catch up with them.

Leadership was a burden. He knew better than the others what would soon transpire. They *guessed* what he would do, but that was not the same thing as making the actual decision. If people died, their fate was on his hands. He had seen too much death lately, and was too old for this sort of responsibility. But the men still obeyed him without question. Had they known that

Lanrik was now the true Lindrath … well, they would obey him too. He had won their respect years ago, and beyond doubt earned more of it in the last few years. He was become a legend to them. And he was a fitting successor.

The king might think he could disband the Raithlin. But they were all brothers and sisters, and they were bonded even closer now after what they had endured. When the time came, they would follow Lanrik without question, and many of them, they younger ones in particular, would join his new Raithlin in Lòrenta. The order would continue, and Lanrik would head it.

Lanrik would be shocked if he knew that the title of Lindrath was officially his. Not just for the new order, but also the old. He had been in a daze in Conhain's tomb. Small wonder after what had transpired there, but the ritual of succession, such as it was, had been carried out. The link remained unbroken between Conhain, the first Lindrath, and now Lanrik. All that it had entailed was a few simple words in the Halathrin tongue, whispered under his breath: *halar, diril* and *Milath*. Duty, honor and love – the center points of the Raithlin creed. And of course they were said in combination with the secret Raithlin hand sign: the thumb pulling down both middle fingers, leaving the two outside fingers standing up to represent the pricked ears of a fox, a symbol of cleverness.

The column wound onward into the depths of the swamp. The path sloped downward, and now from time to time there were wet areas where mud lay to the sides and even some small bodies of water. These were mostly isolated water holes, and well used as wallows by the aurochs. Their tracks were everywhere near here. It seemed that as the land dried up, the beasts had less choice of places to drink and those that existed were frequented more often. It was good to know from a hunter's point of view, but just at the moment Talgin and the Raithlin were the ones being hunted.

A Raithlin behind him spoke. He was one of the youngest in the group.

"I wish this was a real swamp. They would never find us then."

"That's true," Talgin answered quietly. "But we can be grateful for this at least – there are less mosquitoes, and that's got to be a good thing."

The men around him mumbled in quiet agreement. Raithlin spoke little, always listening and avoiding making noise when on a trail. That the young man had spoken in the first place was a sign of nerves. Not that he was the only one. It showed on everyone's face. They all knew what the Witch-queen had done in the past. They all knew that she sought to destroy them now, and would not give up.

Talgin bent low under a long tendril of gray moss that hung down from a gnarled tree branch. A mosquito buzzed around his ear, and he swatted it impatiently. He hoped he was not wrong about them. The men needed *something* to be grateful for. Hope was a strange thing though. It kept people going, even just a whiff of it, but the moment it was snuffed out completely, there seemed little reason to do anything. He felt a bit like that now, and wondered if all this was futile. Was there really any hope to defeat Ebona?

He thought back to what the spirit of Conhain had said. The first king had confirmed that one day the city would fall. Nothing lasted forever. Although he did not say specifically that it would fall now, with Ebona on the throne. But he had practically told Lanrik to go on, even though there was no hope. But how could the city fall? Civil war? Perhaps. That was possible, it would weaken

Esgallien and her enemies might take advantage of that. He had no answers at the moment. But this much he knew: Lanrik relied on him. And they all relied on the lòhren. He must return to Esgallien, for he was the best chance they had to overthrow Ebona and save the city. If it *could* be saved.

Aranloth was Ebona's greatest enemy. But he was not the only one. Lanrik was of the blood of Conhain, and Talgin was sure that she knew it. The same blood that had once defied her, rebelled again. And Lanrik bore the first king's sword. She could call it chance. She could call it fate. But whatever she called it, it would drive a cold shiver up her spine. And so it should. Lanrik was not as other men. Small surprise that he was of Conhain's line. And Erlissa, pretty though she was, had a will of steel and powers of her own. Between them, they were a force to be reckoned with.

Lanrik did not need to be king to defy the Witch-queen. He had done that already. Nor did he need to be king to rally the city around him. It struck Talgin that though the Witch-queen hated all the Raithlin, she hated Lanrik the most, and feared him. This troop of guards following them might have been sent with only one real purpose in mind: find and kill Lanrik. Killing the rest of them might only be a secondary issue.

The more he considered it the more likely he thought that to be the case. Not that it helped his situation now. The guards would fight them whether Lanrik was present or not. And if they prevailed, they would search, or wait for him, should they guess that the Raithlin were expecting him to return to this spot.

All of this just reaffirmed what he had planned. He would not leave the swamp, or even the path through it. They would fight a hundred guards if they needed to. They were Raithlin, and the wild lands were their haunt.

The guards had numbers, but they were out of their element.

A disturbing thought struck him though. What if Ebona had sent some kind of witchery with the guards to help them?

8. The Slithering Dark

The bones within the pit undulated like an angry sea. Some flew up from the surface, catching the flickering lòhren-light for a moment, and then tumbled down again with a dull clatter. A fine powder rose and hung in the decay-scented air. It caught in Lanrik's throat and hindered his breathing.

As suddenly as it began, all movement ceased. The powder drifted slowly along some invisible air current, its flow illuminated like dust in a beam of light that pierced the roof of a dark forest.

Lanrik drew his sword. Erlissa gripped tight her staff.

"What is it?" he asked.

"I don't know," she answered. "Some sorcerous thing – bred, bent and twisted by elùgai. This much I feel. It is *old*."

Lanrik gazed down into the pit. The empty eye-sockets in the skulls of the long dead stared back at him.

The two of them could not wait here, on the exposed ledge, forever. They must venture the narrow path that ran up to the door.

Erlissa came to the same realization. She stepped ahead, leading the way. He followed, now seeing for the first time that bones also littered the path in several places. At least there were not many, but how they had come to be there, he could not guess. Perhaps people had fled whatever lurked within the pit. If so, the growing height of the ledge as it climbed toward the door offered little protection.

They proceeded slowly. They had to be careful of their footing on the narrow shelf, and yet at the same time they dared not remove, even for a second, their watchful gazes from the pit.

They reached the halfway point before anything happened. There was a flash of movement near the surface of the bones. Lanrik caught a glimpse of something black amidst the white, and then he saw the swift turning and revolving of a coiled body, sinuous and immense.

They put aside their fears of falling in the face of greater danger and ran. Yet still they kept a close watch on the pit. They had only taken a few paces before a massive head emerged from the bones.

It was black. Scales gleamed like frosted grass in the dark of the night. Two eyes stared back at them. They were large orbs, slitted and cold, filled with pitiless hatred.

The head turned slightly and more bones fell away to reveal the upper body of a huge serpent. It was a thing of corded muscle, thick as the trunk of a tree. Its back was black but its belly was the red of fresh-spilled blood.

A long tongue flickered, tasting the air for the scent of prey. It reared back suddenly. A shivering hiss rose from the bottom of the pit and echoed softly off the stone sides before whispering down again from the vaulted roof.

More of the body came into view, and yet there seemed no end to its length. Its tail must be deep down in the pit. And the creature must have thrashed it there for now bones bounced and rattled and flew into the air with a renewed cloud of dust. The whole chamber thrummed with an unsettling sound.

The serpent hissed again. Lanrik looked in horror on long fangs. They curved out from the upper jaw, dazzling white, as large as a man's arm and slick with venom. A single drop fell among the churning bones and sudden steam and fumes wafted high into the air.

At that moment the head reared back. The body swayed higher, and the jaws opened wide exposing a vast pink throat that pulsed and gleamed.

The creature struck. Its head shot forward fast as an arrow sped from a bow. Yet it did not try to pierce or rend them with fangs: it spat venom instead.

A stream of foul-smelling liquid spurted through the air. Once again Erlissa anticipated events faster than he. With a flick of her staff she raised a blue shield of lòhren-light.

The venom sprayed into it. The light flickered. Noxious vapor filled the air and made them dizzy. Yet the shield held and protected them from the deadly fluid. Had it not, Lanrik did not doubt that it would have killed them.

Some of the venom slipped past the rim of the shield and splattered against the wall behind them. There it smoked and hissed.

"Take care!" Erlissa yelled.

Her warning was hardly necessary, but he appreciated it.

A moment later the lòhren-light wavered and disappeared. They ran again, climbing higher along the ledge and toward the door at its end. If safety lay anywhere, it was there.

They did not get far before the serpent reared once more and belched poison yet again. Erlissa was quicker this time. Her shield of lòhrengai sprang up well in time. But it was weaker.

The venom drove into it with force. It hissed and roiled against the shield. Blue light flickered and went out. Fluid splashed the stone near their feet; there it blackened all it touched while putrid smoke curled and coiled upward. But neither fluid nor even smoke touched them.

"Run!" Erlissa yelled.

They sped further up the ledge. The door was near now, a massive construction of iron, pitted by rust and age. If it was locked, or barred in any way, they were likely dead.

The serpent reared again. Lanrik stopped running. In one swift motion he unslung his bow, nocked an arrow and sent the shaft winging through the noxious air.

The arrow whistled as it flew. The serpent, jaws agape, dodged to the side quicker than the arrow's flight. The shaft flashed past its neck and sped on to smash into the far wall of the pit. Yet before its flight was halted, Lanrik had nocked another arrow and sent it arcing toward the creature.

This time the serpent was not so quick. The shaft drove through the air, and straight and true was Lanrik's aim. The barbed head sank into the pink flesh of the creature's throat.

The great jaws snapped too, and then they opened again, wide and gaping. Splinters of the broken shaft fell down. And yet, though Lanrik could not see it, he felt that the metal head would not be easily dislodged. The bow was strong and would have driven the arrow deep.

The serpent's reaction proved it. It thrashed and roiled, hissing and spitting. Venom dribbled from its mouth to the bones below. Smoke rose in a sluggish cloud.

Lanrik and Erlissa ran again. He had bought them a little time, though he doubted it would last. The serpent would soon remember its prey, and anger and pain would spur it to attack with greater fierceness.

They reached the door. Lanrik searched for a handle. There was none. He thrust his shoulder against the metal, driving his weight forward, but it did not budge a hair's breadth. He took hold of one of the three slanted struts that formed the drùgluck sign and pulled. Nothing moved.

"We're trapped!" he cried.

Erlissa had no chance to answer. The creature attacked again. It arced its sinuous form high. Its long body glistening black and red. Then it threw its coils among the bones, thrashing and flicking its tail deep within the litter of ancient death. The chamber thrummed to the eerie rattle.

Bones smashed into the wall of the pit, shattering to fragments and puffs of dust, many of them near where they stood at the door. Erlissa straightened. Coolly, she pointed her staff at the creature and lòhrengai sizzled through the air.

A bolt of lightning leaped, striking out from the staff toward the black head of the serpent. Fire engulfed it. Flames swarmed and danced, blue against the black, lighting the whole pit with a feverish glow.

The rattle of bones intensified and then suddenly died down. The fire flickered out. The serpent dropped back into the depths of the pit. It thrashed and swayed. Smoke rose from its head. Venom dripped from its fangs, but it was not dead, or even dying.

It gazed back up at them with cold eyes, blacker than the pit had been before Erlissa's lòhren-light first lit it. There was hatred in that gaze, and an intelligence that considered and calculated.

"It's a thing bred of ùhrengai," Erlissa said. "I can hurt it, but not kill it. It will attack again soon."

Lanrik turned and drove his full weight against the door. Still nothing happened. They were trapped, unable to go either forward or back. And neither lòhrengai nor arrow was strong enough to kill the serpent.

9. A Clear Conscience

Talgin did not ride at the head of the column.

His sight and hearing were not the sharpest in the group, and the vanguard was a place for the best. Yet he still guessed the approach of Arawdan and Arawnus, or at least one of them, returning from their forward scouting before any of the others and signaled a halt.

The Raithlin waited, still and silent. Their faces showed anxiety, and hands rested on weapons: sword hilts, throwing knives and strung bows. No one knew for sure whether friend or foe approached.

The trail ahead was gloomy. It was a thick part of the swamp, and old trees, knotted and bent by time, swayed over the path. And the path had become dry too. There was no lake in this swamp, no vast body of wetlands at its center. In fact, the land was rising and drying out quickly.

Out of the trail-shadows ahead a rider appeared. The figure whistled an old tune long out of favor in Esgallien. Talgin did not need to see the Raithlin cloak to be sure it was one of the brothers – the whistling was enough. It was a Raithlin tactic to identify themselves to other Raithlin in order to insure that no mistakes were made and that weapons remained unused. He had taught the brothers that tune himself.

The rider came down the column, acknowledging many quiet greetings as he returned. He approached, his hood still up and his face shadowed. Talgin was still unsure which of the brothers it was.

The man behind him spoke.

"How did you know that someone was coming?"

Talgin turned and smiled. "My sight isn't what it was, but even a blind man could hear that the crickets in the distance ceased to chirp."

The man shook his head, disgusted with himself that he had failed to notice the same thing. It was a lesson he would not forget, but he was not alone. None of the other Raithlin had observed it, otherwise they would have signaled a halt themselves.

Talgin allowed a faint smile to play on his lips. Age might have blunted his senses, but it had not yet dulled his skills.

The approaching rider drew up beside him. He saw now that it was Arawdan.

"We've found a spot," the Raithlin said.

"I take it that there's no point in delaying and looking for a better one?"

"There might be more suitable places further along, but not by much. Better to let everyone rest first, and then get things over and done with."

Talgin noted that Arawdan was vague about what 'things' needed to be over and done with. He did not blame him.

"You're right, I expect. How far away is it?"

"Not far, but the going is rough."

"Is Arawnus still there?"

Arawdan shook his head. "He went to scout further along the trail and make sure that he could find a way out of the swamp."

Talgin rubbed his chin. That was good knowledge to have, but he hoped they would not need it.

"Take the lead," he said. "We should still have an hour's head start."

Arawdan turned his horse around and went to the head of the column. What sort of spot he and his brother had settled on, Talgin did not know. He would find out when he got there, but he did not doubt that it would be suitable.

As Arawdan had warned, the trail grew rougher. The land continued to slope upward, and what little vegetation there was that resembled the swamps back home disappeared. They were now surrounded by tufted grasses growing along ridges and between outcrops of rock. A forest of stunted and dry-leaved trees overshadowed everything.

Although the land was drying out, and there was much shade, it grew hot. Talgin wiped sweat from his face and felt it dampen his tunic and trickle down his sides.

It did not take them long to reach the spot the brothers had chosen. The column came to a halt and Talgin rode up to Arawdan at the front. Of Arawnus, there was no sign.

He looked around, studying the terrain through the eyes of many long years of experience.

Trees stood to either side of the path. They were not tall, but they grew quite thickly. The ground on the left was higher, the trees covering a rocky slope that ran up to a crest out of sight above. To the right there was also a slope, though not so steep or rocky. The trees grew taller there, but just as thick.

The trail ran through a gully between the two slopes. It was dry, and yet at times, when it did rain, water obviously collected here for the grass grew well. It stood over a foot high, covering much of the trail, but it was mostly dead now, dried and withered by heat. The sun came from before him, and would do so for a few hours yet.

He turned to Arawdan. "The path is wide," he said, "so the guards won't be strung out."

"That's if they ride into it. If they suspect an ambush, they may not."

"That's true. But it's still wide ahead of the gully, and if they don't enter it, we'll have to make them."

Arawdan looked at him grimly, knowing what he meant. "I don't much like the thought of using fire, but this place is perfect for it."

"You and your brother did well. The rest of it will be up to bold hearts and luck."

"Isn't it always?"

"More than most realize," Talgin answered.

He signaled the column forward. "Let's keep appearances up," he said. "It's better that whatever trackers they have with them see our trail continue forward through the gully. When you've gone through to the end, halt them and give them instructions. I'm going to find a place in the middle of the trail to wait."

"Are you going to talk to the guards when they arrive?"

"I'm going to try."

"They won't listen."

"No, but I'll try anyway. I don't like fire either. And if that fails, at least it will help to ensure that they're bunched up in a group."

Arawdan rode through the gully with the Raithlin. What his exact thoughts were on trying to speak to the enemy, Talgin could guess. He would have preferred to spring the ambush without warning.

Maybe he was right, but these guards were also men from Esgallien. They might serve the Witch-queen, but they were still his countrymen. He wanted to avert a fight if he could. And if he could not, then what he said was true. They would bunch up to hear what was said, and that would serve the Raithlin well.

Most of all though, he did not think whoever led the enemy would fail to see this as a place of ambush. The guards might be young, but whoever led them was likely a man of experience.

He trailed behind the Raithlin, and then came to a stop two thirds of the way down the gully. There a knee-high boulder jutted from the ground. He dismounted and sat on it, keeping the reins of his mount close to hand. It was not tied, but would not stray.

He watched the Raithlin as they took up positions. They left their horses in the rear, and came back to the gully. Some maneuvered their way high up the slopes, disappearing from sight even though he knew where they were. A group of men established themselves near the mouth of the gully on the right, and a group of women took up a place opposite them. None were visible.

In moments Talgin almost felt that he was here by himself, alone in the wild with a hundred guards on the way. But he was not. His brothers and sisters would not abandon him. They were ready to fight, come what may.

A breeze stirred, gusting through the gully and across his face. It cooled him down. It also confirmed that Arawdan and Arawnus were skilled Raithlin; not that he needed any special proof of that. The gully channeled air just as much as it did water during whatever wet periods occurred in this strange land. That would serve a purpose – a grim one that he hoped the guards need never discover.

He knew when the guards approached. He read the signs in the wild, and in truth it took no great skill. These men were not Raithlin. They spoke among themselves. Their horses trod over rocks, harnesses jingled, birds called alarms and took flight from trees. Some of these things the guards could not help, and yet for the most part their approach was a shambles. But their lack of skill in such matters did not mean they could not fight. Not only that, with Ebona driving them and the shadow of her menace upon them, they would fight with desperation.

He waited, humming a tune to himself and sitting casually on the boulder. That at least was what the enemy would see. They could not know that his heart raced with fear, or that he worried for Lanrik. Less still would they know that he hoped that their commander was wiser than he seemed. For only *he* had the power to avert the death that would otherwise run like a river of blood through the gully.

There was silence for a time. He knew that their lead riders had spied him and sent word back to the men. Their commander would come to the fore any time soon.

The minutes droned on. There was no noise but the breeze sighing lonesome among the tree branches and the chirping of crickets coming as if from a great distance. Talgin hummed louder, and then broke into a whistle, reviving the same old tune that Arawdan had used earlier.

At length, the commander emerged from the shadows of the trail. He nudged his horse forward slowly. A group of ten men was with him, and they came forward with care. Talgin kept on whistling, watching them carefully and tapping the same tune he whistled with one of his feet that dangled down the side of the boulder.

The group came closer, and behind them the remaining ninety men also came into view. As hoped, they now bunched up and milled restlessly behind their leader.

The commander came to a halt just before the mouth of the gully. His sword was not drawn, but like all the others, he held a shield up high, anticipating trouble.

The captain of the guard looked at him coolly. When he spoke, his voice was one of authority, and though Talgin read wariness in his every movement, there was no fear in his voice.

"The road here was long, Lindrath. But this is where it ends. Give up now, and I promise to escort you to the queen in safety. You will be treated well."

"*You* might treat me well," Talgin answered. "But what of the Witch-queen? Can you say the same of her?"

There was a pause. "I do not speak for Ebona. Perhaps you can come to an arrangement with her. Many have. She rewarded them well."

"You mean that I should betray all that I know and love, including Esgallien, to try and save my own skin."

The pause was longer this time. "That more or less sums it up."

Talgin laughed. "I had always thought that you Royal Guards lacked an ability for plain speech and used instead the double talk of the palace. I see that I was wrong."

"The truth is the truth," said the man. "There is no need to hide it."

"And what is the truth of our current situation?"

The man cocked his head in thought. "That's simple enough. You will not give up, and we will have to kill you."

Talgin grinned and jumped down from the boulder.

"Then come and get me."

The captain shook his head slowly. "Do you take me for a fool? This is a trap. I know an ambush when I see one. You have your men to either side, and you yourself are the bait. We will not go in there. If we must, we will go around and come at you from the heights, or hunt you down if you flee."

"The heights and the trees are no places for horses."

"I have not come to talk tactics with you. Surrender now, or we move on to the next stage."

"And what is that, exactly?"

The captain spoke again, but this time he directed his comments to the slopes on either side.

"I know you are there, Raithlin. I know your number and that this is an ambush. But I will not set foot into your trap. We outnumber you by far, and I offer you this, direct from the queen herself. You may all go free. She will pardon your crimes against the realm, and you will not be hunted any further. In this, you have her solemn guarantee. Moreover, she offers you all a place among the Royal Guard. It grows, day by day, and there not only will you retain your freedom, but you will have privileges and wealth beyond what the Lindrath ever bestowed on you. She asks three things in return. Should you grant them, our business here is done. Otherwise, your time on the earth swiftly draws to an end."

There was no answer. All remained silent save the breeze shaking the branches and rustling a path through the dry grass.

"Well, it seems as though I remain spokesman." Talgin said. "What three things does Ebona wish?"

The captain looked at him. If he was disturbed not to get an answer from the Raithlin, he did not show it.

"Yourself. The traitor Lanrik, and the witch Erlissa."

Talgin waited a moment, and then he raised his voice in order that all might hear.

"Well, Raithlin. What is your response?"

The silence remained unbroken.

Talgin waited long moments, and then spoke again.

"You have your answer. Now, I in turn will make an offer to you, and to all your men. I cannot grant you wealth. Or privileges. I cannot even guarantee your safety. But I can give you a clear conscience. Join *us*.

Fight with us against Ebona. Do what is right for the city, for the people – for yourselves, before it's too late."

The captain stared at him for a few seconds and then shook his head.

"You have nothing to offer." He motioned to his men and they began to back away. "We have time. We will eventually kill you all."

The captain started to back away, but at that moment arrows flashed through the air. They streaked with smoke and fire. And they hit their targets, but these were not men. The arrows landed behind the guards. The withered grass caught fire. The wind took the flames and spread them. Gathering smoke drove into the mouth of the gully.

Arawdan and Arawnus had chosen their place of ambush well. The flames sparked to life swiftly and leaped and danced toward the guards. They seemed disorganized. They looked about in fear, and their horses shied and became skittish.

The flames grew higher as more of the dry grass caught, but the Raithlin were not done yet. A great racket rose suddenly behind the enemy: sticks bashed against sticks, rocks against rocks and the clamor of wild yelling joined with the roaring of the flames.

Some of the guards lost control of their horses. The animals bolted away from the flames and into the gully. As they jostled forward, they pushed many others ahead of them. Soon many had entered the killing ground of the gully.

Talgin drew his bow and fired. Within moments other arrow shafts sped through the smoke-filled air. They came from left and right. They came from low and high. Most found their mark.

Horses screamed with fright. Men cried out. The smoke thickened and roiled through the gully, choking breath and dimming sight. Heat came with it now as the flames ran like a wave, the wind driving them.

Many guards toppled from their saddles. Confusion and fear reigned. Some tried to turn back and face the flames. These were cut down by arrows. Some tried to move to the sides. These also were cut down by the unerring skill of the Raithlin.

The captain gathered some few men around him and charged Talgin.

Talgin sprang up on the boulder again, waited a moment, and then drew his bow once more. The smoke stung his eyes. Tears marred his sight. But three arrows he sent winging in quick succession, and three men, one of whom was the captain, dropped from their saddles.

Men yelled in confusion, swords flashed, but only arrows and throwing knives answered them. It was a massacre.

The flames drove down the gully. Riderless horses bolted to safety. Talgin mounted his own, which had also grown skittish, but he calmed it and moved up the slope and into the trees away from the smoke.

He looked back, ready to shoot again, but there was no need. The guards were dead. They lay in the gully, the fire racing over their corpses and speeding down the channel. But at its far end it began to slow. There was less grass there, and the banks opened up so that the wind diminished and drove the flames with less force.

Already he saw Raithlin leaving their hiding spots and working to put out the flames. And that was well, for nothing drew the attention of eyes, friendly or unfriendly, like smoke in the wild.

The Raithlin stamped with their boots and used bushes and branches to beat out the flames. It was hard work, but the patch of dry grass was burned out and the flames were already dying without their help.

Talgin looked back with a stony gaze into the gully. So much death filled it, all so needless. And the Witch-queen lay behind it all. He gritted his teeth in anger. There would be more of this before it was all over. Much more.

But a reckoning was coming. Ebona would pay for every life that was lost.

10. The Price of Malice

Lanrik stared at the iron door.

The three slanted struts forming the drùgluck sign unsettled him. Above them was a small viewing window, only one foot by one foot across. Iron bars ensured nothing could pass through it, though the window was too small for that anyway.

A new thought struck him, and it disconcerted him more than the drùgluck sign. He guessed the purpose of the window. No doubt Assurah had brought sacrifices to the serpent. He had forced them through the door, secured it behind them, and then watched as the creature devoured them, growing strong on the lives he fed it.

He felt deeply sickened. And then fear for himself and Erlissa set his heart fluttering. But a cold anger washed over him a moment later. He would not die down here. Nor would he fail in the quest to free Aranloth, for the lòhren was the best chance to defeat such evil in Alithoras.

He peered through the window. The room beyond was dim and he saw little. Standing on his toes he looked down at the bottom of the door's other side.

It was secured at its base by an iron bar thick as his arm and bent over at its top to form a convenient handle for hands to lift it, though it was beyond his reach from this side. The bolt dropped deep into a hole bored into the stone floor, and the strength of twenty men would not force the door open.

And yet the discovery gave him hope. But even as he considered the situation the serpent hissed behind him, and he knew it was about to strike again.

He left their defense to Erlissa and did not look. He trusted her. She would do what could be done to protect them, just as he would do what could be done to get them out of here.

The serpent attacked. He drew his sword, but did not turn to face the creature. Instead, he took it by the blade and slipped it hilt first through the bars of the window. Assurah, long dead now, could not stop him as he once might have hindered any efforts of his victims. He lowered it until the crosspiece of the hilt fitted beneath the bent top of the bar and pulled upward.

He strained, but nothing happened. The bolt had rusted and centuries of dust and grime had clogged the hole. It held the bar fast.

Blue light flickered behind him. Foul liquid sprayed the nearby walls, and he braced his muscles in fear of the sudden sting of venom or fang. But Erlissa had saved them again, though he heard her groan behind him.

Once more he strained to lift the bar, and this time he felt movement. He tried again, and suddenly the bolt slipped up in the hole and he drew it high. The bar was heavy, and he took care that it did not drop again. When its bottom was clear of the hole he pushed against the door.

It opened with a screech. Rust and debris fell from the hinges. He continued to push and it swung more freely.

He let the sword drop to the other side with a loud clang, but his voice rang out louder still.

"Come through!"

Erlissa dived past him. He followed. Turning and pushing his weight against the door once more, he drove it back into a closed position. He saw vague movement through the barred window, and then heard a hiss and the rattling of bones. The serpent rose up, higher even than the door, and it was about to strike again.

He rammed home the bolt, grabbed his sword, and then rolled to the side.

It was none too soon. Venom sprayed against the door, and some splashed through the barred window to land on the floor. There it seethed and bubbled. Black smoke curled up from the stone.

They looked at each other in the near dark.

"Well, you took your time," Erlissa said with a weary grin.

He winked at her. "When I take a girl out somewhere, I like to show her an exciting evening."

"Exciting isn't *quite* the word I'd use."

"Exhilarating, then?"

"No. I think not. And just how many girls have you taken out?" She shook her head and then continued. "No. Don't tell me. Anyway, I don't think there *is* a word for what just happened back there." She cast her gaze at the door. "At least we got past it in the end."

Lanrik stood up. "Yes, but the problem is that we have to get past it again on the way back. And I fear it'll be *really* angry the next time."

Erlissa sighed. "First things first," she said. "For the moment, we'd better find our way to Aranloth."

Lanrik looked ahead as the blue light at the tip of Erlissa's staff flared weakly.

The room was dark and shadowy. Dust lay over the ground and grime streaked the walls. There was very little here, the main feature being a winding staircase ahead of them.

They walked toward it. Though the floor was covered by what once had been well-fashioned flagging, the walls were of natural stone. They were still beneath the actual tower, and this area was either carved out of the living rock or else the tower was built upon a system of caves.

Erlissa confirmed his thoughts. "The tower straddles this bedrock," she whispered. "And in both the bedrock and the tower foundations above I sense the striving of elùgai and lòhrengai. It seeps through the very stone, and some mighty spell, cast no doubt by Assurah when he raised the tower, binds the stones together. The elùgroths seek to unravel it and bring the tower down. Aranloth prevents them."

Even as she spoke Lanrik saw the hairline cracks that ran through the walls. The staircase showed them too, for it also was carved from the bedrock.

"We'd better hurry," he said.

He sheathed the sword of Conhain and took the lead up the stairs. They left boot prints behind in a layer of gray powder that covered everything. It was not the dust of time, but rather a fine film that had recently fallen from the ceiling. He saw it even now drift slowly in the blue light of Erlissa's staff.

They circled several times, following the winding staircase. It was hard to tell when the natural stone ceased and the great quarried slabs that formed the tower's foundation began, but by the time they reached the next level everything was man made.

The room here was round. It was large, and full of scattered tools such as hammers and tongs. Smoke darkened the walls all about them and blackened the roof.

To one side was an ancient furnace, and near the center stood a great anvil. Rust stained it. Spider webs covered it. Time made it look decrepit, yet still it dominated the room.

This place was a smithy, and beyond doubt the shazrahad sword that he had taken from the enemy was forged here. And though that forging was thousands of years ago, still in his mind's eye he saw a shadowy figure, bent, sweat-soaked, hammering, twisting red hot metal and beating it into a sword blade while sparks scattered around him in the dark. He heard even the hiss as the new blade was tempered in great barrels of water to the side. These now had half rotted. Only tarnished metal hoops held them together.

He shook his head and kept walking. The first keg was empty. The inside of the second was darkened by a stain and at its bottom lay hardened sludge. It smelled too, a foul scent that reminded him of the serpent's venom.

The staircase led upward again, now hugging the encircling walls of the tower.

They came to the next floor. This was once the entrance. A door still stood there, a thing of massive iron just like the one below. It too showed a drùgluck sign, but this time it was formed by three slanting depressions in the metal rather than struts. There was no way through it. The crown of the tower now lay in rubble on the other side. Just as well that way was blocked, for the elùgroths were gathered on the other side, though not so close that they might succumb to any attack from above by Aranloth.

They moved up the staircase, but Erlissa grew dizzy and swayed. He reached out, putting an arm around her shoulders, and steadied her.

She gritted her teeth. "Such forces!" she said. "They swirl all around us!"

"I don't know how Aranloth has defied them for so long," Lanrik answered.

"I'm beginning to understand," she said. "Elù-Randùr is among them, but he does not lend his power to the assault. He believes Aranloth is caught in an inescapable trap, and for that reason he sees no need to hurry. I think he enjoys sensing Aranloth falter, and feeling him become more desperate."

"Well, his malice might just end up costing him yet."

"So I hope! Anyway, let's go on."

Her dizzy spell passed and with each upward step she became surer on her feet.

It was a long way to the top. They grew weary of the climb. Nothing relieved it, for the tower was the same on each floor. A door stood at every level, each one broken down and rotted, and the rooms within held nothing save the dirt of the ages. Elugs or Azan had long since looted anything valuable, if indeed any such things had ever been there. Now only dirt and vermin filled the rooms.

In some were windows, and though Lanrik wanted to look out to see where the enemy was, and what they were doing, there was a risk that they would see him. Anyway, the best view would come from on top.

They must be close to that now, at least he thought so. The rooms were getting smaller as they wound up to the narrowing pinnacle of the tower. Suddenly, the stairs thrummed beneath them and they felt the very tower begin to sway. Just as soon as it started, it stopped, but Erlissa's face was pale.

"Hurry!" she said.

They started to run and discovered that they were closer to the top than they thought, for in just a few strides they came out through a door onto the turret.

It was nighttime. Stars twinkled above, but swathes of clouds covered many patches of the sky. He could not see bright Halathgar, and that disturbed him for he had always taken the Lost Huntress as a sign of good luck.

The air was still, even this high up, and it was bitterly cold. He shivered, and shivered again when he saw Aranloth.

The lòhren sat on the floor near the broken remains of the merlons. His white robes, wrapped tightly about him, were dirty and tattered. His head rested in one cupped hand, and his face, now bearded, appeared haggard and drained of color. His other hand gripped his staff tightly. Tremors ran through his body and his fingers twitched.

He looked up and saw them. Long moments he stared, bewildered by their presence, or dazed by the effort of holding off his enemies for so long. It was the first time, even through many desperate situations, that Lanrik had ever seen him at a loss.

At length, his mouth worked, and words, dry and raspy, came as though from a man who had not spoken for many years.

"How?" he said. "How did you get here?"

Erlissa walked to him, and then bent low so that the elùgroths would not see her from below. She put an arm around his shoulder.

"Don't worry about how," she said. "Let's worry about what next, instead."

11. The Waiting Dark

Lanrik bent down and moved stealthily toward the fortifications while Erlissa spoke with Aranloth.

All that was left of the many merlons that had once ringed the tower as a crown were broken foundation stones, jagged and sharp like shattered teeth.

Peering through one of the many gaps he smelled the lingering odor of burnt stone where lòhrengai had scorched the surface.

It was some time in the middle of the night. Away to the west, he saw the dark shadows of other mountain peaks running off into the distance and out of sight. Lights twinkled in some of the valleys far below, nestled within the deep night that gathered at the base of the mountains. He heard the bleat of sheep on the wind, and a faint whistle as cold air drove over the top of the peak that rose, dark and craggy, above the tower.

Down below he saw the elùgroths, darker shadows amid the night. They sat in their wedge, black staffs gleaming beneath the sky, all pointing at the tower. He caught the faint drone of some chant that they muttered while the stars wheeled above and their power strove against Aranloth's.

Erlissa helped the lòhren to stand. He was unsteady on his feet, but between his staff and her arm around him, they managed well enough.

Lanrik had seen all that he needed to. The elùgroths showed no sign of knowing that a rescue was taking place. He crawled over to the others before he stood up beside them.

Aranloth's haggard face turned to him. "You should not have come."

"Shush," Erlissa answered before he could respond. "You would have done the same for us."

Lanrik grinned. It was a strange thing to see: the great Aranloth, shushed by a young girl. Of course, she was not just *any* young girl.

"Let's go," she said. "It's a long way down and the sooner we start the sooner we'll reach the bottom."

Aranloth straightened. Their presence seemed to give him fresh hope. It also brought back a faint stirring of his usual strength.

"What of the creature that lurks below?" he asked. "And how did you get in? There's no way in or out of the tower. At least, so I thought."

"We'll have to fight our way past the creature. That's our only path to escape."

"It's strong," he said. "I felt its presence, but I did not see it. I sensed no way out beyond it though."

"Obviously not. But you're not a seeker. And just as well none of the elùgroths are either."

Aranloth shook his head slowly. "Then I'm a fool. A way out was before me all this time."

"It still won't be easy. As you say, the creature is strong. It's a thing of ùhrengai, bred, bent and twisted by Assurah."

They started to move down the stairs. Lanrik was worried. Aranloth's resistance to the elùgroths was all that preserved the tower. His strength, whatever was left of it, was devoted to stymying their efforts. He would be of little help, or none, when they reached the pit. And yet somehow they must get past the serpent.

They reached the first room below the tower's high pinnacle.

"How many tunnels run beneath the pit?" asked Aranloth.

"It's a maze down there," Erlissa answered. "They're dangerous and unexplored. Assurah would have known about them, but other elùgroths obviously never learned their ways. The knowledge died with him."

Aranloth shook his head doubtfully. "Dead? So we all thought, but I'm no longer sure." He pointed with his staff at the open door before him into the topmost room of the tower.

"I learned things in there. Things that made me question everything. Assurah was no ordinary elùgroth."

Erlissa stared at him. "What do you mean?"

"Later," he answered. "For now, we must hurry. My strength falters."

They moved down again. Lanrik looked into the room as they passed. There was little to see. Desks and chairs rotted on the dirt-covered floor. Shelves, fallen down and broken, cluttered the room. And there were books too. Many of them. Most appeared wet and moldy, though some seemed better preserved. This was likely Assurah's study, though what Aranloth could have discovered within it after thousands of years and the depredations of water and vermin, he did not know.

They continued down the stairs. Erlissa supported the lòhren on one side, and he on the other. It took them a long time, and all the while Lanrik considered different plans to evade the serpent. None would work.

They must rely on the same method to get down and out as they had to get up and in, but this time the creature was ready and awake, and they were tired. Erlissa had barely got them through last time, and his arrows had not helped much. They annoyed the thing, but not much more.

At length, they reached the smithy. There they rested a few moments. Lanrik looked around. Once more he went to the tempering barrels. The sludge at the bottom of the second one intrigued him. Working on a hunch, he drew forth an arrow and dipped the barbed head in the muck at the bottom. If that was the serpent's venom, it could do no harm to try and shoot it with its own poison.

Erlissa and Aranloth approached.

"Is that what I think it is?" she asked.

"I think so."

She frowned. "I see what you're trying to do, but the serpent will likely be proof against its own venom."

Lanrik shrugged. "Probably so, but it does no harm to try."

They moved down the stairs to the last level before the pit. He held the arrow carefully, being sure that it did not come into contact with anyone. He saw Aranloth study it intently, though whether for fear of the venom or some other reason he did not know.

At the bottom of the stairs they approached the great iron door.

"Tread carefully," Lanrik said. "There's venom on the floor."

He had sudden doubt if the substance that he had dipped the arrow in was venom. The floor here was corroded by it as though tongues of intense flame had licked it, and yet, if the substance in the keg had been venom, how could the wood resist its corrosive power?

It was a good question, and he had no answer other than that wood was not stone.

"Exactly what manner of creature is it?" Aranloth whispered.

Erlissa glanced nervously at the door while she answered.

"It's a great serpent, massive and strong. Its back is black, its belly scarlet. Time has not diminished it, rather it has grown cunning through the ages and perhaps, being drawn from ùhrengai in the beginning, has learned how to use that power to sustain and strengthen itself."

The lòhren looked grim as they moved to the door. Carefully, Lanrik peered through the grilled window. He saw nothing, for the pit was dark. Nor did he hear anything, not even a whisper of sound among all the dry bones. The serpent could be close, or not, and he would not know.

He shrugged at the others, and then put his hands to the iron bolt that fixed the door in place. Looking up at them, his eyes questioned if they were ready.

Erlissa nodded curtly. Aranloth took a deep breath and straightened as though preparing himself.

A long moment Lanrik waited. He did not wish to enter the pit again. And yet there was no other way.

With sudden force he lifted the bar and then pulled the door open. The iron hinges grated. A flash of blue lòhrengai burned at the tip of Erlissa's staff, and then they were through and shambling along the ledge that led down the side of the pit.

Erlissa took the lead. Her black hair trailed behind her, and the walnut staff gleamed with power in her hand. Aranloth came next. He moved quickly, though what effort it cost him Lanrik was unsure. He did notice a strong tremor beneath their feet and knew at once that the lòhren diverted some of his great focus on the struggle with the elùgroths to the benefit of their own predicament.

For his own part, Lanrik nocked the arrow to his bow and came up the rear, eyes roving below for any sign of the creature.

He saw nothing but the mass of white bones in the pit of death. There was no movement, no sign of the thing at all. Had it settled once again beneath them? Did it coil there quietly in the dark and rest in order to heal the wounds inflicted upon it? That was possible, but Lanrik knew it was not the truth.

If it was not in the pit, where then could it be? With growing certainty he realized. It was before them on the ledge, hidden in the long shadows cast by Erlissa's light. And they were running straight toward it.

Even as he grasped that thought he looked ahead beyond the jostling forms of Erlissa and Aranloth, and caught sight of it.

The black-skinned serpent lay lengthwise along the ledge, its great tail disappearing in the dark. Its whole body was flattened, pressed down low to the stone. It held its head low and still.

"Stop and duck!" he cried.

The other two obeyed instantly. At the sound of his voice the creature stirred. Thirty paces ahead of them, its head lifted. Black eyes bored into them, malice drove through the air like twin spears.

Lanrik drew his bow and prepared to shoot, though what good it would do he was not sure.

12. A Wind of Dust

Lanrik let fly the shaft.

Even as it sped from the bow, Aranloth gave a flick of his staff and a spark of white lòhrengai shot from its tip to join the arrow's flight.

The serpent reared, fangs bared. The arrow took it below its lower jaw and stuck there. It did not penetrate deeply, driving only some six inches into the creature's muscle-hardened flesh. It reared back, angry but unaffected.

With a sudden hiss and strike, it spat venom at them. A blue shield sprang up. Erlissa stood tall behind it. Aranloth leaned on his staff and panted. He had already spent what little strength he had on the spark, and whatever he had tried with that had failed.

Lanrik slung the bow over his shoulder and drew Conhain's sword. It glittered in the eerie light. When the shield faltered, he would charge past the other two. If lòhrengai and arrow-shaft could not kill this thing, perhaps Halathrin steel could.

The blue shield flickered. He stepped forward, but suddenly the long arm of the lòhren reached out and gripped his arm.

"Hold!" Aranloth commanded.

Lanrik could not break free. The lòhren's grip was surprisingly strong, yet every moment that passed was a lost opportunity, for the serpent would renew its supply of venom, and the time to attack was just after it had depleted it.

But Aranloth held him firm, and in a moment Lanrik saw why. The arrow still jutted from the creature's flesh. It was too shallow of a strike to do any real damage, and the venom on the barbed head, if venom it was, had at best been a faint hope. Yet the spark of lòhrengai that Aranloth had sent with it caught on the shaft and grew. White streaks ran along its length, and they sought the arrowhead and the venom covering it. When they found it, sparks flew from the serpent's flesh, spurting out of the wound. The red skin blistered, and then blackened from within.

The serpent thrashed. Its long form smashed into the wall and then much of its body swung out over the pit. There it hung and whipped around wildly while white flame erupted from its flesh. A moment later it slid into the pit, coiled and thrashing, the great tail twisting and spraying up bones.

"Run!" cried the lòhren.

Erlissa streaked ahead in the dark, the light of her staff bobbing madly. Aranloth stumbled forward. From where he drew his reserve of strength, Lanrik did not know. But he was near the end of it and would likely not reach the bottom of the ledge. Not swiftly enough anyway, for already the serpent seemed to cease its lashing and to gather itself.

Lanrik came up beside the lòhren, took him in his arms, and lifted him. In that way they sped down the ledge.

The lòhren was heavy. Though he appeared like an old man, he weighed like a warrior, dense with muscle.

Erlissa had drawn ahead, but she paused a moment and waited for them to catch up. In those moments the serpent rose again. The arrow had broken off or burnt away, and the skin of its neck hung in blackened shreds. Dark blood seeped forth and heavy drops fell onto the white bones below. The serpent hissed, a sound filled with hatred and pain. Aranloth's lòhrengai had worked. It had reacted in some way with the venom, that being a thing stemming from ùhrengai.

Its long tongue darted forward. The creature reared higher until it towered above them, black eyes boring with hatred and its mouth agape. Aranloth's fire had burned deep, for now the pink flesh of its inner throat was also blackened, but fresh venom dripped from the sword-like fangs.

Erlissa attacked again. Lòhren-fire spurted from her staff, but she did not strike at the serpent. Instead, the bolt shot down into the pit and tore through the debris of death. Skulls rolled. Bones toppled. The pit seethed and rolled like an angry sea.

Lanrik saw what she was doing. In a moment, it worked. The support beneath the serpent shifted. The creature toppled forward, half toward them, but also down and deeper into the pit, below their level. It would rise again, but they now had a few extra moments to flee.

The bottom of the ledge was in sight. Beyond were the tunnels. Even if they reached them, the serpent would follow. And yet in the narrow confines its movements must be slower, and it could not rise high to spit venom far.

They made the end of the ledge. The serpent rose behind them. Lanrik stumbled forward, the weight of Aranloth dragging him down.

"Run!" the lòhren yelled with urgency, and Lanrik struggled forward with a new burst of speed.

Even as he surged ahead, he felt a change. He was not sure what it was, but Aranloth gave a long sigh and suddenly went limp. Lanrik feared he was dead, but it was not so.

The very air now seemed different. Erlissa ceased her flight and looked back.

"Get down!" she screamed.

Lanrik knelt down. A grinding noise, low and deep, pressed against his ears. Powder cascaded over him, and then with a groan and roar the ceiling of the pit behind them collapsed. The bedrock stone, the man-made foundations and the tall tower all drove with immense weight into the hollow beneath it. One moment he saw the serpent, writhing and twisting toward them, the next all was dark in a wind of dust and rock that blew strong as a storm-gale into the tunnel.

They lay still for many long moments. It was hard to breathe, and though the light shone bright from Erlissa's staff, it was hard to see.

This much was clear. Aranloth had withdrawn from the struggle with the elùgroths, and the tower had crumpled. The fate of the serpent was harder to know. It might be dead. It might be buried alive, yet working, sliding and slithering its way free. Lanrik did not want to wait to find out.

He scrambled to his feet, and Aranloth now stood beside him. The lòhren let out another sigh, as though the weight of the world had been lifted from his shoulders. In a way, it had been.

The tremors in the earth subsided, but the choking dust did not settle. It remained difficult to breathe, and they staggered ahead in search of clearer air and escape.

Gradually the dust thinned, and Erlissa's lòhren-light shone forth with increasing brightness. Tunnels and caves opened up to each side of them, but she guided them truly until they reached once more the underground lake. There they paused.

"What is it?" Aranloth asked. He was still weak, but his voice was steady and strength was returning to him.

"There was something here on the way up," Lanrik answered. "It dwells in the water and it attacked us."

"There's no sign of it now," Erlissa said.

Lanrik saw nothing either. "Then we'd better go forward while we may. It might be that all the noise and rumbling scared or confused it."

"Perhaps," Erlissa said.

She did not sound confident, and yet there was nothing else for it but to move ahead.

They stepped onto the narrow land bridge. Erlissa led, Aranloth followed and once more Lanrik came up the rear. He fitted another arrow and kept his gaze fixed on the surface of the water.

It was not as still as earlier. Rock fragments and dirt fell from the roof and disturbed it. Several times he started to draw the bow in order to shoot, for he saw movement, but on each occasion he soon realized that it was nothing alive.

They crossed the narrow land bridge. It was very wet; not just from where the creature had caused a wave to roll toward them before, but all along its length. Down here, even this distance from the collapsed tower, the lake must have broken over its shores as the earth moved.

They came to the far end without incident. It seemed as though the creature was scared and chose to leave them alone, or else the lake was connected to other underground reservoirs and it had fled further along one of these to avoid the tumult.

They rested on the far side. "Luck must be on our side, for once," Lanrik said.

Aranloth gave him a tight grin. "Luck is *always* on your side. Don't you know that?"

"It doesn't seem that way sometimes. It definitely didn't when the serpent attacked."

"Yet you got through. And out of the midst of a ring of elùgroths you brought me forth – the both of you. It can't have been easy, but you did it. You need luck for that sort of thing. Some are dogged by ill fortune all their lives. Others, like the two of you, have a way of landing on your feet. Even the serpent was good luck, in its own way. If not for its presence, the elùgroths would have learned of the tunnels beneath the pit. And then they would have secured that path and no rescue would have reached me."

"You have a strange way of looking at things," Lanrik said. "But I see what you mean. Yet tell me this? How good will our luck be with the elùgroths? Will they think you dead and buried beneath the tower? Or can they sense that you still live by some art of sorcery?"

Aranloth thought about it a moment. "They'll be suspicious. Too suddenly I gave up the battle with them, and they'll use elùgai to try and find my body. Minute by minute, as they fail in that task, their doubt will grow."

"And then?"

"And then they will think on it. The serpent must somehow live, and no sacrifices have been made to it for a long time. They know it's there, and they will consider next how it obtains food, and that will mean that it has a way out from the pit. And if so, I may have gone that way. They will know it for a truth when they fail to find my body."

"Then we don't have long before they mount a search."

"No," Aranloth answered. "But I don't think they'll be that quick either. They'll be very tired. Only Elù-Randùr among their number is fresh."

The air was still full of choking dust, but it was lessening. They soon moved on, Erlissa in the lead. She retraced their steps from earlier in the night.

They came to the cave of bats, but it was strangely quiet. The light at the tip of Erlissa's staff flared a little brighter.

"They're all gone," she said.

They did not linger. The air was hot and oppressive, but it grew swiftly cooler as they went ahead toward the exit. They found the tunnel had partly collapsed in places, but the debris did not block it. They were able to move through, crawling carefully over piles of broken rock.

Finally, they reached the crevice that led outside. A long while Lanrik stood within its shadow, peering out and listening. It was still dark, but he guessed dawn was coming. The fresh air felt good on his face, and he breathed deeply of it.

The horses were still there, dim shapes in the dark. It appeared that no one had found them, nor would he have expected that to happen, but it was well to be careful.

They had far to go today, and time was against them. At some point the elùgroths would realize their prey had escaped and would come looking. Likely, they would rouse the Azan to search as well, so the three of them would have to risk riding during the day. That was a dangerous thing to do in a land seething with all manner of enemies.

He drew his sword and stepped out of the cave. The horses twitched their ears and looked at him, but he still saw no sign of anyone else. He went to them, Erlissa and Aranloth coming behind him. There was no lòhren-light now.

They untied the horses and mounted.

"Dawn is not far away," Lanrik said.

"It will be a long day," Aranloth answered. There was a note in his voice, not one of fear but of sadness. "Elù-Randùr will not give up."

13. Drums and Silence

They had not gone far down the trail when the drums began.

The beat was slow. The rhythm did not change. It was a deep thrumming that rose from the foot of the mountain and swelled around the high peaks. Even as it did so, other drums answered from afar. Soon many valleys up and down the Graèglin Dennath voiced their own deep-throated song.

Lanrik was in the lead. He stopped and listened before turning back to Aranloth.

"What does *that* signify? Has the hunt for us begun already?"

"No," the lòhren said. "At least, if it has begun, the drums are no part of it." He paused, his expression grim. "You have heard them before."

Lanrik knew their sound. Once heard they were never forgotten.

"Elug war drums," he said. "But why beat them now?"

Aranloth continued to look at him. His eyes were deep pools of ancient sorrow, and he made no answer.

Lanrik thought about it, and then the slow realization came.

"They prepare for war. Too long a weak king has sat upon Esgallien's throne, and strife tears the city apart. Soon the hosts will march against it."

Aranloth gave a curt nod. "I have seen some of their preparations from the top of the tower. At times the elùgroths would taunt me also, asking how it felt to be trapped while their armies made ready to cross Galenthern and destroy all in their path."

"Well, we'll bring back word to Esgallien and warn them," Lanrik said. "We can travel much faster than their army."

Aranloth's expression did not lighten. "Are you forgetting Ebona?"

"I forget nothing about her. But surely, now that she sits upon the throne as queen, it would be as disastrous for her as everyone else if Esgallien fell."

"Perhaps. It's hard to know what she wishes. Her mind is ever mysterious."

"I saw her in Caladhrist," Erlissa said quietly. "I saw her when she had gathered great power in that ancient place. And having tasted the beginnings of what she could become, she will never turn aside from that desire. I saw a look in her eye that I will never forget. She would become as a goddess – and she would sacrifice every life in Esgallien to achieve it."

Aranloth looked as somber as Lanrik had ever seen him.

"I fear Erlissa is right. Just as in Conhain's time, she would cast a net of witchery over whole armies and draw power off the slaughter. She will wax and grow, and care not if Esgallien falls. There are other cities. And who could stop her from usurping their rule?"

"Then we shall stop her first," Lanrik said, "before that comes to pass. And then we'll defend Esgallien."

"Those are two separate tasks, of which neither will prove easy," Aranloth replied.

Lanrik grinned. "No, they won't. But we found the Lindrath and brought him out of the city to the safety of Galenthern. That will serve as a good start."

Aranloth whistled. "Well done! That gives me hope!"

107

The lòhren considered this new information a moment, and then his eyes narrowed.

"I sense there's more. Tell me."

Lanrik slowly drew the sword of Conhain. It glittered palely in the growing light, the faint rays of the new sun running along its length and gathering like golden sparks at its tip.

He tested its weight in his hand and was about to explain what had happened in the tomb when he noticed the lòhren's expression.

Aranloth sat tall in the saddle. His gaze was bright eyed. It took in all that it saw of the pattern-welded blade, the shimmering edges and the jeweled hilt. There was astonishment on his face, for the sword was a thing crafted with the skill of the Halathrin. No other people could match it. It was a deadly weapon of war, but it was also a work of surpassing beauty, for the immortals crafted everything they made with the deep love and skill that came of life unending.

The lòhren showed more than astonishment: there was recognition too. His eyes widened after the first few moments, and then he gave a final nod. He had seen that blade before. He had seen it in Conhain's own hand. He had seen the first king of Esgallien draw it and charge, though he was dying, into the battle that birthed the realm. Such a blade could never be forgotten, even if a thousand long years stood between sightings.

"It fits," Aranloth muttered. "It all fits together. I learned more of the shazrahad sword in the tower. I discovered more of the prophecy infused into its blade, and then many things made sense that had puzzled me before."

The lòhren looked at him with wise eyes, though there was a certain appraisement there also.

"You are of Conhain's line. That's why the shazrahad sword drew enemies and problems about you when you held it. It seeks to fulfil the prophecy that if ever a king of the north bears the blade the kingdom will fall. And yet, though you are of the line, you are *not* king and the prophecy smolders rather than catches fire."

Lanrik was astonished in turn that Aranloth knew all this without explanation, and his surprise must have showed.

"How else could you get Conhain's sword, if you were not of his line?" the lòhren asked.

Lanrik nodded. "Did you know any of this before?"

"No. I didn't. But I knew there was more going on than I could understand, and that a reason lay behind it. Now, between us, we have the answers."

Erlissa stirred. "Not all of them. What did you mean earlier when you said that Assurah may not be dead?"

Aranloth ran a hand across his eyes as though trying to wipe away some unpleasant memory.

"Assurah was dark," he said. "Dark even for an elùgroth. He spoke seldom, even with his own brethren, keeping his plans and secrets to himself. That much was to our advantage, otherwise the elùgroths would have learned more of his tower and what lay beneath. He mastered many things of which they knew nothing, both in thought and deed. He gathered about himself powers that they would not understand, and he used them as his body faltered and death approached." Aranloth spoke ever more softly, as though fearful of being overheard. "I do not think he died in the end. Nor do I think he still lives. I cannot be sure what happened. His books were vague. Few would understand them. None if they did not know certain lore that survived the dark days after the fall of the Letharn Empire. He was suspicious of everyone, especially his own kind. He told them nothing, but there were clues of what he intended in his notes. He infused some part of *himself* in the shazrahad sword. He *is* the prophecy. His spirit has taken another body, one of enduring metal rather than flesh. He wanted to live forever, or at least long enough to realize the destruction of the north."

Lanrik felt suddenly strange. He was not sure what it meant that Assurah had infused a part of himself into the shazrahad blade, but whatever it signified he knew this much at least: he had carried that sword around, and the elùgroth's malevolence, working ill will, had gone with him every step of the way. And yet that was only a part of it. The sword had also been imbued with a more recent power.

"What of the lòhrengai that you drove into the blade?" he asked Aranloth. "How does that influence things?"

"A good question," the lòhren answered. "In truth, I don't know. But I feel this – it seemed right at the time, otherwise I would not have offered to do it. Given a lack of evidence one way or the other, I'll trust my instincts that it'll work out for the good. I also think the sword has a role to play in upcoming events, though what, or even how, I cannot say."

Lanrik did not ask him more. If the lòhren had seen some vision, he was not saying, but it was more likely that he had just some vague premonition. When, and if the time came, he would say more if he could.

"One last thing," Lanrik added. "The spirit of Conhain told me that the sword would be both blessing and curse."

At that, Aranloth raised his eyebrows. "That's interesting. I'll think on it. This much only will I say now. I know where Conhain rests, for I built that tomb. And I know what it would take to rouse him from his slumber.

You, Lanrik, are favored. There are others of Conhain's line, and yet he gave his sword to you, that is clear, for otherwise you would have died trying to take it. He chose you above all others, and if he gave you the sword, he means you to wield it, rather than the shazrahad blade. That says much to me, but it does not say the shazrahad sword will remain unused in Lòrenta. My heart forebodes it will yet play a role. One we did not foresee, though it be pivotal, for the words of the dead are as great a gift as a Halathrin blade, even if they are likewise two-edged."

They continued down the trail. Dawn blossomed. It lit the land like a swift fire, and the chill of the night was replaced by warmth that already showed signs of turning into a hammering heat.

After a good while they approached the Azan village. A long time they waited in the shadow of some rocks near the water pools, but they saw no sign of anybody. Yet people had been here. There was evidence that shepherds had brought their animals to water, for the rocks and stones all around were slick. But the place was quiet now.

They refilled their water bags, and then let the horses drink. All the while it was eerily quiet except for the beat of the drums that thrummed away in the distance. There was no other sound, save for sheep and the high-pitched call of hawks that hovered in the hot air seeking prey, or that sped arrow-like as they hunted among the high ridges.

When the horses had taken their fill, they moved on. The village was ahead, but it too was quiet. It appeared deserted, but it would not be so. The three of them put up their hoods, but they had little chance of seeming as Azan riders. Yet pass through they must, and Lanrik kept a hand near the hilt of his sword. He rode with

111

confidence, and though he wanted to scrutinize the huts for signs of watchers, he did not. It was better that they rode as though they belonged here and did not care who saw them.

No one emerged from the huts, and he heard no noises either. He felt sure they were marked though, and that would go against them when the elùgroths came searching.

They moved ahead. Even if the men had gathered elsewhere to prepare for war, there must still be some left, especially the infirm and elderly.

Aranloth seemed to read his thoughts. "Those who are left are likely herding and hunting," he said when they were out of earshot.

"Let's hope they herd and hunt far from the trails that we must follow today," Lanrik answered.

He said no more, for they came to the horse yard. There he looked around in all directions, but still seeing no sign that they were watched, he dismounted and opened the gate.

Aranloth seemed surprised, but then for the first time since seeing him on the top of the tower the lòhren smiled, and many lines of care and fatigue fell from his face and did not return. He had seen his roan, and it whinnied to him in greeting.

Lanrik fetched the horse, and the lòhren dismounted and ran his hands along the beast's flanks and patted his withers.

He turned to Lanrik. "For this, I owe you. The two of us have traveled far together, and I thought I had lost him forever."

Aranloth swapped his saddle around to the roan and led the other horse by hand. There was still no sign of any Azan, and they continued onward.

The sheep pen was empty. It did not look like there was much to graze anywhere in the Graèglin Dennath mountains, and yet it was surprising how well they seemed to fatten even in those dry conditions. There would be places too, hidden in folds of the land, where the pasture was lusher and sweeter than others. No doubt the remaining men had taken the sheep to some such place, but whether the road was visible from it was anyone's guess. He must assume that it was, and that if they had not been seen yet, they soon would be.

The shoulder of the mountain was on their right, rising to many high ridges, and to their left the valley opened up. The bottom was deep and far away over many steep slopes. Smoke drifted upward, and the air was hazy with heat.

There were many villages down there, and Lanrik got a sense of how vast the lands of the Azan were. For here they were halfway along the range, but it extended hundreds of miles to either side. Southward, beyond the range and into the flat deserts of Grothanon, few reports ever spoke. It was said that the elugs dwelled mostly on the southern slopes of the ranges, but they also inhabited the interior. If so, the enemies ranged against Esgallien were vast in number and toughened by their land.

The morning wore on, growing hotter and hotter. Lanrik was wary of all the silence and stillness. Nothing moved apart from their own slow-plodding horses. Eventually they reached the boulders where he and Erlissa had hidden. There he called a halt, for he saw something disturbing.

The tracks of alar horses were on the dusty road. That much was expected, but there also he saw many boot marks, iron-shod and deep.

"Elugs have been here," he said. "This far up the road they came, but no further. Whether that means they hunt us still, or have given up the chase, I cannot say."

Aranloth looked puzzled, and Erlissa explained their clash with elugs down at the base of the range.

"That they followed you is a given," the lòhren said. "But elugs and Azan do not live together, though they may dwell near one another. I would say that they pursued you, but having reached this far, they would go no further into Azan lands. That does not mean, of course, that they do not lie in wait somewhere below against the chance of your return."

Lanrik sighed. It was just one more enemy that he did not need, and one more reason why he may not live to bring word back to Esgallien of the impending invasion.

14. Foreboding

Lanrik looked out to the north. Home lay in that direction. But immediately ahead was Galenthern. Not the green and lush plains that he knew so well, but still something with which he was familiar.

The grass was baked brown by the sun, and today was a hotter day than most. The plains shimmered below him. He did not see as far as he was used to from the tor near Esgallien on a clear-aired winter's day, but he could still see well enough, and what he observed made his blood run cold.

Wherever he looked he noticed signs of a gathering army. In some of the nearby valleys, still under a night-like shadow due to their steep sides and depth, he observed camped hosts.

They were elug hosts. They infested the valleys and gorges, and they poured along roads and trails like ants returning to a nest. When their numbers were swollen enough, they would burst like a flood over Galenthern and rush toward Esgallien.

The elugs were not alone. There were riders among them: white-robed Azan. In this war not only would they serve as the leadership of the elug army, they would fight themselves. He saw also lethrin. They were few in number, but their size and black battle dress ensured they stood out.

"This must still be only a part of their preparations," he said.

Aranloth stirred beside him. "The Graèglin Dennath is vast," he answered. "But these same scenes must be taking place for hundreds of miles to left and to right. It's the greatest gathering of our enemies in many hundreds of years."

A long time they could have watched, for the incessant activity and ever-growing numbers drew the eye, but they did not.

"You don't see them," Lanrik said. "But there are Raithlin on the plains. They are not that far away, and I wish to be with them. I've had enough of the Graèglin Dennath."

He nudged his mount forward, and the others followed. There was not much of a trail, and soon even that disappeared. It seemed the Azan preferred their dry mountains and ventured seldom onto the plains.

He recognized few landmarks, for when he and Erlissa had ventured up the trail they had done so at night. But from time to time he saw something that he knew, and using that as a guide, he deliberately veered from the way that they had followed on the first journey. He had not forgotten the elugs. They could be here somewhere, waiting, only now they had more help ready to hand. It was best to try and avoid them.

Despite his fears, he saw no enemies. As they went lower, the elug-filled valleys were no longer visible. Nor could he see much of the plains. The heat rose in waves and the air was full of fine dust.

What he did see was movement higher up, near to where they had begun their descent. But it was not a rider. It was an animal, and it leaped from boulder to boulder and among the shattered rocks of a high and inaccessible ridge. It moved with seamless grace, despite its precarious footing. It was goat-like, though larger, stronger, and fleeter of foot. And it had great horns, twisted things, beautiful but likely deadly. It paused, perched delicately upon the crest of a rounded boulder, and looked down at him even as he looked up.

"It's a talnak," Aranloth said. "Rare these days, for the Azan hunt them, though the hunting is dangerous in the beast's favored high places. More Azan die than talnaks, but they value the meat and hide, and the horns even more."

They continued down toward Galenthern. These mountains were nothing like Lanrik's home, nothing like what he was used to, but there was still beauty in the land, and it was growing on him.

He glanced at Aranloth. "Did you plant the seeds that the Guardian gave to you?"

"That I did. Not all in one place, but not that far from here is a large valley. It's deeper than most, and the soil is richer. One day, when the time is right, they'll sprout. If they survive the chances of time and fate, perhaps they'll grow, set seed and start to spread into other valleys. So the Guardian wished, and you can be sure that they're not quite ordinary trees. They'll be strong, and spread well, and perhaps even bring back some of the beauty this land once held."

Lanrik did not answer. At that moment a horn blast tore the air. It was in the distance, but even so they sensed the urgency of it.

"A talnak horn," Lanrik said.

"The hunt is up," Aranloth answered. "The elùgroths, or at least those spared from commanding armies, begin the chase, and Azan will be with them."

Erlissa looked grim. "It'll be a long day, and there's nowhere for us to hide. We must ride in the open, but the Raithlin are nearby."

Lanrik took a tight grip of his reins. "Then let's start, and let the followers follow."

117

Aranloth nudged the roan into a trot, and they all surged forward. The lòhren's look was dark though. He seemed preoccupied, and Lanrik guessed he was thinking of Elù-Randùr. That the elùgroth would pursue was a given, and he would not be pleased. Yet again Aranloth had escaped one of his traps, and his plans had failed once more.

They sped ahead. The day drew on. The hot sun hammered down, drawing sweat from riders and mounts. A trail of dust billowed in their wake, but it was of no matter. There was little point in trying to avoid dust clouds when the riders who caused them were in the open for all to see.

The sun fell into the west. Long shadows groped down the sides of the mountains, reaching after them as though the Graèglin Dennath was unwilling to let them go. In the distance, higher up on the slopes where the sun still shone, a group of riders was visible. They were Azan, and they hastened down the trail. But one elùgroth at least was with them, and even at that distance Lanrik saw the wych-wood staff lifted and pointed toward them menacingly.

"Elù-Randùr," Erlissa whispered. As she spoke, the night took hold, and the last dim rays of the sun faltered. Yet still they sensed a blackness that was not night. It gathered as a cloud behind them, and a wind drove it down the mountain. From its shadow there would be no escape. At least, so Lanrik felt, and he could not shake off the thought.

They rode into the night. The hot air dissipated. The cool, dry air that replaced it comforted both mounts and riders, yet they still must pace their race properly. If they over rode, their horses might break down before they reached the waiting Raithlin. If they under rode, the pursuers would catch them before they reached safety.

Not that the Raithlin offered much protection against an elùgroth, especially one of the great ones such as Elù-Randùr. Only Aranloth might defy him, but he was still weak, if gaining strength by the hour.

There were many signs of the gathering southern army. Lanrik read the marks of numerous hooves and many iron-shod boots in the withered grass. He did not need the skill of a Raithlin for that. The marks were obvious even at night.

Out of the dim reaches of the darkness behind them the talnak horn sounded again. It was a warning. It signified that the pursuers did not give up the chase. Night might slow them, but it would not stop them. They would stay on the hunt.

Lanrik turned east. Here he saw the tracks of several riders, and he followed them. The others did not question him; they trusted to his skill. But skill would avail them little here. Their tracks would be harder to read, but the pursuers need only follow the whole group and watch for the point where three broke away again. There they would turn aside themselves and continue the chase.

Yet still the tactic offered something, for at night such a breakaway trail would be harder to find, and it would slow them a little as they would not want to bypass it. That could make all the difference, for an hour or two of rest would freshen their own four horses and add speed to their legs if the pursuit quickened during the next day.

They saw little. A long way behind them were campfires. They sprang to life in a blaze, and there were many of them. If elugs and Azan were gathering like that over the length of the Graèglin Dennath their army would be massive.

For the first time Lanrik felt doubt. He doubted they would escape Elù-Randùr without a fight. He doubted their ability to overthrow Ebona, and he doubted that Esgallien, even warned and prepared, could survive against the tide of war coming to drown it.

He felt fate at work, the same fate that had been averted when all this began. There would be no Lathmai this time though, and no slowing down of the army. It would not work a second time, nor would it matter if it did. What most needed doing was the overthrow of Ebona, for something greater even than Esgallien was at stake. Should her power wax on the sacrifice of entire armies, should she grow until her strength was unassailable, all Alithoras would fall before her.

15. Long have We Waited

They rode well into the night. Sometimes they led the horses by hand to ease their burden, sometimes they trotted them and occasionally they pushed them hard where the ground was smooth and soft.

They stayed on the trail of the other riders for some while, but Lanrik knew that he could not do this for long. Traveling eastward was not getting them closer to the Raithlin, or to home.

The night was getting old when he found some suitable ground to change direction. The grass was dry and short, the earth hard and void of the type of rocks that might turn beneath a hoof and leave evidence of their passing.

He slowed their pace to a walk. "Time to turn north," he said.

They followed him off the trail. The horses left very few signs, though a keen eye would mark them. A long while he kept his mount to a walk, ensuring that the hooves made no deep imprints even when the earth grew softer again.

They held the horses at a walk for nearly half a mile before they trotted again, and the night grew cold about them. The stars shone bright above, and from somewhere far away came the long and drawn out call of an aurochs. It was a reassuring sound. Galenthern was a place that Lanrik knew, and he had friends here. He only hoped that they had not been forced to abandon the arranged meeting place.

Dawn was not yet come, but it was approaching when they settled down to rest. Lanrik led them to a grove of stunted trees. It offered little cover, for the trunks were half-dead and the branches bare of most of their leaves. But it gave shelter from the sun and a degree of protection from prying eyes.

When they had dismounted, rubbed down their horses and fed them a little grain, Lanrik sat down wearily and looked at the lòhren.

"How long do you think we have?"

Aranloth gazed southward, as though his eyes might penetrate the veil of night.

"Not long. Perhaps only a few hours before we see them. They'll have good horses – and Elù-Randùr won't spare them."

"But even the best horses have to rest."

"That's so. But we'd better eat now and get some brief sleep. We'll risk not having a watch, I think, for there'll be no time to rotate a guard. I'd say we have until mid-morning at best."

It was a cheerless breakfast of dried meat. They ate the leathery strips quickly, tough ribbons both smoky and salty, with their eyes turned to the dark bulk of the Graèglin Dennath and the shadowy grasslands before it. When dawn came, the sun shot fiery color across the muted plains.

After that, they slept, if sleep it could be called. The heat started again, though it was not so bad as yesterday. Flies were a nuisance, clinging to hands and faces. Only pulling up their hoods gave relief, but that made them hotter. And all the while the sense of foreboding that had started when they came down the mountains continued to build.

They rested little more than two hours. Lanrik woke, or at least stirred from a troubled doze. He found that

Aranloth was already sitting up, his back against a tree and his gaze scrutinizing the plains.

Lanrik did not ask him if he had seen anything. Erlissa was still asleep, and he did not want to wake her. And if the lòhren *had* seen anything he would have woken them already and they would now be riding.

He moved over to a tree close to the lòhren and took up a similar position to watch. He saw nothing but the long line of the Graèglin Dennath stretching out: gray, barren and smoke-hazed. To left and right as far as he could see it remained the same.

Although there was no activity, he knew much was happening beyond his sight. Elugs, Azan and lethrin were all gathering, and soon they would come forth. It could not be long either before Elù-Randùr and his band approached as well. The three of them rested in peace just at the moment, but surely this was now one of the most dangerous places in Alithoras.

Erlissa stirred, and though she stayed where she was he did not think she was asleep any longer, just dozing.

He kept his gaze southward, looking for any sign of the enemy, but he spoke quietly to the lòhren.

"Tell me, Aranloth. I still don't really understand why the spirit of Conhain said that the shazrahad sword was both blessing and curse."

Aranloth twisted his staff in his hands as though trying to find a comfortable grip.

"Should you hold the sword," he said, "it will speed the prophecy, even if you are not the king. That is a curse, for it may still bring the ruin of Esgallien. And yet, look at Conhain's life. All that he ever knew and loved was lost. But on the back of that tragedy, something great arose – Esgallien. And the city has lasted a thousand years, all the while growing grander and more influential. But should it be lost, might not something

123

else rise from its ashes, even as the city itself arose from chaos and battle? Might Esgallien's fall not lead in some unforeseen way to a defeat of our enemies even as it thwarted their progress into the north for all the time since Conhain died?"

The lòhren paused, deep in thought. "For myself, I don't know. But the dead don't look on life with our eyes. Who knows what they see? And if Conhain envisioned a blessing in some manner, then it could well happen, however strange it might seem to us." Aranloth stilled his restless hands on his staff and continued. "I think in this matter that there is no right action, and no wrong action. We must simply trust to fate, or at least in Conhain's words, and the history that we know which gives truth to them."

Lanrik thought about it. He still had no real answers. He wondered if there were any. For anything. Yet all a person could do was what they considered right at the time. Even if the consequences were beyond any foresight.

They rested some more, but did not sleep. Each half hour was a great benefit to them. The horses would freshen up, while their pursuers would be tired before any chase began.

Somewhere in the distance he heard a nudaluk bird. If ever a sound reminded him of home, it was that – or the call of an aurochs. It was a good sign too. The birds favored timbered areas, and he knew he was getting close to where he had left the Lindrath and those who remained of the Raithlin.

They did not have long to go now. Either Elù-Randùr would draw near to them, or they would leave before the pursuit caught up. He waited a few minutes longer, savoring the rest, and considering how the current situation reminded him of how all this began.

Mecklar was long dead, his treachery found out. So much had changed since then. Lanrik had discovered the world was a different place from what he had previously thought it. He wondered if the future ahead of him from this point was as different as the future that his earlier self had never expected.

His musings were broken short. There was movement on the plain. He could not tell exactly what it was, but it seemed to be a group of riders.

Aranloth had seen it also. "Time to go," the lòhren said.

Erlissa got up quickly. She had not been asleep. Her face still looked weary, and surely so also did Aranloth's. It worried him, for he feared Elù-Randùr would catch up with them sooner or later, and there would be trouble if that happened. The sort of trouble that only lòhrengai could fight. But if the two of them were not strong, the fight would fall back to the Raithlin, and many would die.

They did not ride their horses straight away. They led them by hand, allowing them a chance to warm up before being ridden, and to study their gait to ensure no lameness had developed while they rested.

As they did so, the riders behind them came into clearer view. A dust cloud hung over them, and there were flashes of color and bright steel beneath it.

There was little doubt that it was their pursuers, and that was confirmed when the talnak horn blew again. It was dim from all that way away, a whisper on the wind that drifted over the miles to their ears. But it was a promise: *We see you. We chase you. We do not give up.*

Lanrik mounted his steed, but he did not kick it into a gallop. They trotted forward, not giving in to panic, but pacing themselves. The horses were still tired, but they had much yet to give. More than their pursuers who were not as fresh.

Ahead, the plains looked much the same as they did in every other direction, but Lanrik knew where he was going. He did not get lost. Once he had been somewhere, he knew how to get back there, and there were landmarks that he saw that the untrained eye did not.

Soon a fringe of trees came into view. It was only a smudge on the horizon, barely visible, but he headed straight to it.

"The swamp," Erlissa said.

"How many Raithlin are there?" Aranloth asked.

"Too few. Only twenty-one. A small remnant of the one hundred that there used to be. And too few to fight off an elùgroth as well as the Azan."

Aranloth gave no answer.

The riders behind them grew closer, and Lanrik finally picked up the pace. Their horses surged across Galenthern, and the swamp grew closer.

"I smell smoke," Erlissa said.

Lanrik could not, but he did not doubt it was there. That was a problem, for the Raithlin would not light fires, at least he could see no reason for it, and it worried him. Something else was going on, and it was likely bad. Yet there was no point worrying about it. He would find out what the smoke meant soon enough.

They sped ahead. The brown grass flew beneath them. Their pursuers dropped back, but they did not disappear from sight.

Ahead, the swamp loomed. Lanrik saw nothing out of place. Nor did he expect to. If the Raithlin were there, they would not be visible, and yet the three of them approaching would have long since been marked. And the pursuers also.

He swung around a fraction to the west, for that was where he had last seen the Lindrath, and where the Raithlin were supposed to be waiting. It was also the origin of the trail that led into the swamp, and that was important. If the Raithlin were not present, then hiding in the swamp would be essential, and trying to force a way in from the sides would be slow and difficult.

The grass greened a little. The land sloped down, barely perceptibly. They were come to the swamp, and hoary trees sprang up in a sudden wall. The trail was visible a hundred horse strides ahead, dim and dark, an arch into another world. But it was a world that Lanrik was familiar with, and the Azan were not.

They soon came to a halt. There was no sign of the Raithlin. They turned and looked back at their pursuers. A second group had joined the hunt. They raced in from further to the west, but an elùgroth was in the first and closer group.

Erlissa spoke. Her voice was quiet and grim.

"It is Elù-Randùr," she said. "I would know him in pitch night with a mile between us."

"Yes," Aranloth answered. "It was he that tracked me to Assurah's tower. It is always him."

Erlissa closed her eyes. She swayed a little in the saddle. She spoke again, her voice now thin and distant, her eyes remaining shut.

"You will battle him today," she said with finality. "Before the sun sets, one of you will die. I see the fight now. It blazes in my eyes brighter than the sun."

Aranloth showed no reaction, but he answered.

"He and I have both known for a long time that a battle was coming. He was one of my best students, before even the Camar came eastward. Long have we known each other. Long have we waited. Perhaps the student is now stronger than the master. Perhaps not.

But if I die, you must still return to Esgallien. On you, much will fall, for you are now a lòhren. Alone or aided, you must help the people. Promise me."

Erlissa, pale and trembling, opened her eyes.

"I promise."

16. Like Ancient Kings

Lanrik studied Aranloth.

The lòhren still looked tired, but now he also appeared preoccupied. A great cloud of anxiety hung over him. Perhaps it was the likelihood that he must fight the elùgroth. He would know that in such a battle he would not only risk his life but also the future of many lands besides Esgallien. If he perished, it would be an incalculable blow to Alithoras.

There was more though. Overshadowing the obvious was something less clear. His earlier words had hinted at it. Elù-Randùr had been a student. Aranloth had known him well, and they might even have been friends. He would dread any confrontation, for in such a combat he must either die or kill someone who had once meant much to him.

Lanrik sighed and let his gaze fall to the ground. There, he saw something that he did not like.

"A column of riders has come this way," he warned the others. "And recently."

Erlissa followed his gaze. "We came this way ourselves with the Raithlin. Are you sure they're not our own tracks?"

"The marks are confused. I see our old trail. And I see by the length of the strides that at least one rider has passed over them swiftly afterwards. But there are other tracks. More recent, and far more numerous."

"Who do you think they were?" Aranloth asked.

"I cannot tell. Perhaps Azan. Perhaps Royal Guards."

"Either is bad news," the lòhren said. "But there's nothing for it. We must enter the swamp and be careful."

Lanrik looked southward at the oncoming riders.

"You're right. But being careful will slow us down."

He did not wait for any response. Instead, he urged his mount toward the dark arch that began the trail through the fringe of trees. He drew his sword and went forward slowly. If there was some ambush prepared it would likely be sprung sooner rather than later. But either way, the three of them would be caught between enemies behind and ahead. He wished desperately for some sign of the Raithlin, but they may have been forced far away, or even killed.

He entered the swamp. Immediately, it grew darker. The air was clammy and stifling. There was a brooding atmosphere to the place, and now he smelled smoke himself. It was stronger within the protection of the trees where the wind could not take it and spread it over the plains. Something had happened here, and the Raithlin were surely part of it.

They were going too slowly, and their enemies would catch up rapidly. But he could not help that. He studied the trail and watched for any hint of an ambush. He feared every shadow, every rustle of leaves, every narrowing of the trail where the trees gathered densely about them. But nothing happened.

He urged his mount ahead at a slightly faster pace. The tracks of many horses were now quite plain in the dirt of the trail. They all headed into the swamp. None came out. That could be taken as good or bad. Either way, the smell of smoke grew stronger.

They went onward for perhaps an hour. The smoke hung heavy in the air. The swamp was quiet, except for the sound of their pursuers. They must also slow down in here, but they still hurried at a faster pace than Lanrik.

The enemy feared no ambush, but very soon now Lanrik faced a choice: speed up and travel recklessly, or abandon the trail and attempt to hide. It was not something that he would normally consider in a swamp, but here, the land was not so wet as he was used to.

He rode on the edge of the trail, seeking a place where they would not leave any tracks, though he had not yet decided on this course of action. As he did so, he heard the yelp of a fox.

There was no movement, and no further sound, but the yelp had come from somewhere close by, and he came to a standstill. The others waited quietly behind him.

Lanrik suddenly grinned. He made the same yelp himself, only he gave two of them. He felt the stares of Erlissa and even Aranloth bore into him from behind. They had not seen him do that before, and the noise was so lifelike that it even seemed to disturb the horses. They shuffled nervously. But the reason for his strange behavior soon became apparent.

The grass ahead and to their left stirred, but no fox came into view. A man rose up, bow in hand. And he wore something they all knew: the Raithlin cloak.

"Well met, Arawdan," Lanrik said.

"Well met indeed." The man's gaze went to Aranloth. "I see you've gone and done it again. No one really expected you to come back, especially with the lòhren, but you've surprised us once more."

Lanrik raised an eyebrow. "So little faith? Anyway," he gestured behind him as he spoke, "I was only a helper this time. Erlissa did the real work."

Arawdan grinned. "That, I can believe," he said. He started to unstring his bow.

"I would leave it as it is."

Straightaway there was a change in the other man's manner. He stood straight and tall, and his face was grim.

"You are pursued?"

"Yes. And they're close. An elùgroth rides with them also. How far away are the Raithlin?"

"They should be here within minutes. I wasn't scouting far ahead."

Lanrik looked around at their surroundings. They were in a small glade that offered clear room to fight, if necessary. The trees were dense to either side, which would prevent them being surrounded. Also, the track sloped upward at this point, and that would give the Raithlin an advantage. He just hoped that Aranloth was strong enough to deal with the elùgroth. He was recovering, but his ordeal had been great and it was possible that he might be outmatched at the best of times. He glanced at the lòhren, but Aranloth spoke before he could ask any question.

"Here is as good a place as any," Aranloth said. "This contest will be between me and Elù-Randùr. If I win, those with him will not seek to fight you. If I lose, then you had best flee."

Lanrik turned back to Arawdan. "We'll rest here and wait, but I don't think we'll need to wait long."

It was true. Already the sound of harness came to them down the trail over which they had recently passed themselves. But at the same time, though much more quietly, the Lindrath and the rest of the Raithlin appeared. They were on horseback, and he noticed at once that they had already fought a battle. He saw bandages and pained faces, but a quick count proved to him that all were accounted for.

There was no time for talk. He, Erlissa and Aranloth dismounted. The lòhrens lifted their staffs. He drew his sword.

Behind them Arawdan spoke quietly to the Lindrath, and the Raithlin formed a wall. They had only just taken their positions when the Azan appeared. The second group of riders had joined the first, and they numbered double the Raithlin. At their head rode Elù-Randùr.

The elùgroth sat astride a black horse, and his cloak, dark as a nighttime shadow, hung from his tall form over the animal's flanks. His head was hooded, but there was a gleam of pale cheeks and the hint of a deathly gaze. It raked over them like an icy wind.

The alar horses were lathered with sweat. Their heads hung low and several straggling riders came to a stumbling stop at the rear of the group.

The Azan were hard men, weary after their long ride, but they gripped their tulwars in tight hands, and they had the look about them of warriors who were keen to fight.

The Raithlin sat upon their horses behind Lanrik, still but ready. Aranloth now leaned on his staff. He looked as any old man, yet Lanrik sensed some of the power that he held veiled. He shifted his gaze back to the elùgroth, and a chill stabbed him in the heart. Elù-Randùr was looking directly at him.

He understood why legend told that men swooned, or even died, in the presence of one of the great sorcerers. *He* did not veil his power as did Aranloth. He used it as a weapon, for he reeked of menace, and it issued from him like cold air blowing across a frozen river.

Nothing stirred in the swamp. No animal called. No bird sang. A deep silence lay over the land like a shroud of fear that stilled all life.

Lanrik felt an urge to turn and flee, but he knew that if he did so his legs would fail him and he would collapse, helpless, to the ground. Yet as he quailed beneath a growing weight of terror, something stirred in his heart. His spirit rose. It pulsed through him in defiance. He stood taller and stared back at the elùgroth.

At just that moment, Aranloth spoke. His words were couched in an antiquated form, a ceremonial way of speaking that befitted converse between two men who had walked the world in days beyond the memory of mortals. Old he seemed, but his voice was rich and smooth. He spoke not loudly, but by some art of lòhrengai all that he said flowed like a river over the Azan and into the swamp beyond.

"Thou hast come, Elù-Randùr, lòhren that was."

The elùgroth twisted his cowled head to look upon him.

"Verily. And death rides with me. Thou shalt not escape."

Aranloth sighed. "Must we speak of death? We, who once walked the land together and laughed for joy in better times?"

Elù-Randùr hissed. "Say it not! They were not better times. I have found my true master. I serve a power greater than thou, greater than thou canst dream. I am content, thus."

Aranloth gazed at him. "Is that so? It seems to me that anger, hate and mistrust ride with you, rather than death."

"It is not so. Death alone I bring," he paused and pointed his wych-wood staff at Erlissa, "I bring it to her also, and to thy ragtag group of skulkers."

"It need not be so."

"Enough!" cried the elùgroth. "I came not to parley, but to kill. The long-awaited hour draws nigh, the long-foreseen doom arrives. Today, I shall leave thee to rot like carrion in the swamp, play for the wild beasts."

"Thou art bent on this fight?"

"It is fated. Thou know that as well as I."

"Then so be it. I will fight, if fight we must. But dost thou know that fate is the weakest power here? It commands me not, nor, I think, thou. We could part here. We could make our own destiny. For though fate has brought us to this very place, we are masters of our own actions, not it."

Elù-Randùr sat silent. His face remained hidden, though Lanrik knew he would have read doubt there if he looked upon it. It was in the elùgroth's posture, in the slow breath that he sucked into his lungs, in the tilt of his head. A waiting silence listened from the gloom all about them. The future of Alithoras hung in the balance. Then slowly, Elù-Randùr drew himself up. His grip tightened on the black staff. He laughed, a hollow sound, void of mirth.

"Thou speak, but all I hear is the rattle of dead leaves on the winds of change. The eons have tarried, but swift will they fly after thy death, old man. Thine hour is passed. Mine is beginning. Thy death is near, and those with you. They shall fight, even as we, and doom take you all!"

Aranloth did not move. His head was bowed and he leaned upon his staff as though it was all that propped him up.

"As you wish. We will fight. But these others, either Azan or Raithlin, have no part in it. Let it be just you and me."

Elù-Randùr looked at him coldly. "I care not, except for the witch. But if the others are here when you lie at my feet, I shall send them to oblivion."

Aranloth straightened and no longer leaned on his staff. He seemed taller, greater, more kingly than an emperor. His glance was keen with wisdom and with sorrow, but determination sharpened it further. He stepped forward. A glancing ray of light struck silver off the diadem that he wore.

Elù-Randùr dismounted. He held his black staff with pallid hands, blue-veined and sickly. In the west behind him, the sinking sun seemed as a crimson ball on the horizon. It struck red flame across the sky. The elùgroth lifted his staff.

It occurred to Lanrik suddenly that this was more than the end of a day. It was the passing of an age, and Alithoras would be different hereafter.

Red fire swirled among the heavens, and dry leaves lifted up from the swamp, turning, circling, running an ever-thickening ring around Aranloth. A bolt of fire arced from the roiling sky and flashed among them, igniting them in a whirlwind of flame.

Aranloth stood calmly. He pointed his staff at the elùgroth. The flames licked near to him, but never touched him. Suddenly, the trees in the swamp behind blew and bent with the force of a gale. The burning leaves, red and bright, leapt at the elùgroth.

Elù-Randùr bent and swept his staff low across the earth. Dust lifted from beneath it, thick and heavy, rising now high into the air. The flame met it, swirled, and then the dirt denied it air and snuffed it out. The swamp was no longer lit by a red and eerie light, though strange glints and gleams flickered in the sky.

And although the red fire was extinguished, still the dust cloud swirled. It gathered together, hardened, turned into hail-sized rocks. Elù-Randùr drove the point of his staff forward and the cloud darted at Aranloth like a swift flock of birds: beaks and claws razor sharp.

Aranloth lifted his staff. A mist of water rose from the earth. The air stank of swamp water. It formed a veil, which coalesced into a very wall. The rocks struck it. They hissed. And then they dissolved into mud at the lòhren's feet.

Elù-Randùr now summoned wind. It blew fiercely, moaning among the treetops. It groaned through the swamp like a living thing come to wreak destruction. What sorcery was intended, Lanrik did not know. Aranloth forestalled it. He surged forward, but made no counterattack of lòhrengai. Instead, he struck at the elùgroth's head with his staff.

At the last moment Elù-Randùr blocked the blow. Aranloth, undeterred, lashed out with a fist. He moved with the speed of a warrior and his knuckles cracked against Elù-Randùr's face with a sickening thump.

Elù-Randùr staggered back. He lifted his staff. A surge of red fire shot from its tip. Aranloth raised a silvery shield. But it seemed that he was too slow. The red fire smashed into it, knocking him down and engulfing him.

Lanrik felt sick to the pit of his stomach, but suddenly the lòhren rose. He who should have been burned to ash, stood proud and tall. A white light flickered around him. His diadem glittered as though it were a diamond-studded crown.

They faced each other like ancient kings, coming to a meeting at the border of their vast realms.

"Turn aside," said Aranloth. His voice was calm. "Renounce thy service to the dark. Join me in the fight against it."

"No!" cried Elù-Randùr. "Not ever!"

"The dark will lose," Aranloth continued. "It has nothing to fight *for*. Not really. You know that now. The longer you live, the more you realize it is not about you.

137

It never was. It is about helping others. Let us sit side by side and learn again. Let us exert ourselves for the benefit of Alithoras. There is much, very much, that we could achieve. Otherwise, the crop you sow will be the harvest you reap."

A moment Elù-Randùr hesitated. Little of his face was visible, but the cowl had fallen back somewhat and Lanrik read a flicker of emotion. He saw something strange, like the memory of distant days pass over the man's face. The world went still again. He heard or saw nothing else, captivated by Elù-Randùr's expression. A moment it lasted, and then was gone.

By way of answer to Aranloth's words fire spurted from the wych-wood staff. It drove at Aranloth. The lòhren pushed his staff harder against the ground. Fire wrapped around him, coated him, roiled and circled as a cavorting whirlwind. But mostly it gathered around the vertical staff, and then suddenly it shot into the earth.

The flame was gone. All was silent. Both lòhren and elùgroth seemed spent. Elù-Randùr gazed at his one-time mentor with hatred. Aranloth, strangely, looked sad. Tears wetted both of his cheeks. And then the earth trembled. A rumor of power woke from deep below.

Elù-Randùr looked around, bemused. Too late he realized that his own power had been sent back to him. Red flame flickered like darting hands that clawed at his feet. He stumbled, dropped to his knees and the staff fell from his grasp. He tried to rise and leap away. Instead, the flames pulled him lower. He crumbled to the ground. His hands caught alight as he tried to push himself up.

Fire and smoke were all about him. He struggled to heave himself upward. For a moment he began to rise, but then his strength failed and he sank down.

He looked at Aranloth, hatred in his eyes.

"The dark is coming, old man. The dark is coming! Thou, and all thou lovest, shall be swept aside!"

Fire engulfed him. It ran, red and flickering, over his body. The cloak flared. The hood rolled back. Even his pallid face was alight, burning like a white candle shot through with red sparks.

Elù-Randùr tore at the earth with blackened fingers. Soon, he stopped moving, and died.

Aranloth whispered an answer to his last words. "It has already begun."

What he meant Lanrik had no time to think.

He stepped forward. The elug bow in his hand, an arrow trained on the closest Azan who seemed to be their leader.

"Go! Go, or die as well."

The Azan hesitated. But his heart was no longer in the fight. The alar horses sent up ash from their hooves as all the warriors turned. With a final look at what was left of Elù-Randùr, their expressions unreadable, they sped away.

Aranloth fell to his knees. Erlissa stepped close and kneeled beside him. She placed an arm around his shoulders. It was then that Lanrik understood the lòhrens words. Those we love hurt us the most.

17. The Gleam of Madness

It was a long night near the edge of the swamp, but dawn found Lanrik and his companions heading north.

He thought as he rode, for the group spoke seldom as they hastened onward. They were somber and quiet, having seen much, and been through much that made them pensive. They knew also that darker days lay ahead.

The southern army must be near ready to march. The escape of northerners from their land would hurry their preparations, but even so, he guessed that the enemy would not trail them by many days anyway. It gave very little time to organize a defense for Esgallien, but overthrowing Ebona was the main concern. If that were not accomplished first, nothing else would follow.

Doubt weighed on him as it rarely had before. There was, as yet, no plan to defeat the Witch-queen. Nor were the southerners launching a raid or sortie, but rather an attack on a scale that far exceeded anything that Esgallien had seen for hundreds of years. Even the ford offered no sure protection against it. Nor the city walls, if it came to that.

Full well did he realize the importance of Conhain's sword. It would give hope. It would rally soldiers. But he was no Conhain, either in military skill or as a leader of people. The task was above him, but to no other had the sword been given. Conhain had passed it on to him, and with that gift had come haunting words: *One day the city will fall.*

He feared for the place that had long been his home. He feared for tens of thousands of lives. And he feared to be a figurehead in the struggle for a nation to survive. But more than those things, he feared not trying, for if he quailed, who would take his place?

His thoughts shifted to the Lindrath. Talgin seemed different, but he could not tell exactly why. More and more he had been deferring decisions to him. It had now reached a point where the Raithlin came to him for orders, and he gave them, though grudgingly, for it was not his place. But the Lindrath was withdrawing, and it was no accident. Whether he wished to see how he would lead, or tested him, or wished him to gain experience, he did not know.

Erlissa was thoughtful. She remained preoccupied, as though trying to puzzle out a solution to all of the problems Alithoras faced. The responsibilities of a lòhren had changed her. Now, she took thought for the future and planned. He in turn increasingly trusted to instinct and allowed the future to show itself when it was ready.

Each day passed much as the others. The sun arced through the sky from dawn to dusk, and they rode. At night they camped, lighting small and smokeless fires, telling tales in hushed voices and sleeping with a good watch.

Galenthern grew greener as they went. The east often threatened rain, with clouds piling up deep and dark, though they did not deliver any downpour. Yet it grew cooler. For not only did they travel north, but also the seasons were turning, heeding nothing of the quests of mankind, the battles of lòhrens and elùgroths or the fate of nations. Spring had come and gone, summer was waning and soon autumn would arrive. Already the nights showed a promise of winter.

It was late for an army to move, but winters were not harsh in the south, and they were still mild in Esgallien, though snow was certain to fall. He was not sure if the city would survive to see it though.

****

Brinhain lifted his weary head. His chains rattled, and his wrists chaffed where the thick iron cuffs secured him.

He wished he had not moved. Pain stabbed through his left side, and he felt the most recent of his wounds open afresh. Warm blood seeped from it, adding yet another stain to his filthy clothes.

All about him dozens of other prisoners moaned, or stared vacant eyed, already dead in spirit. For he was in a dungeon, though it was like none that he had heard tell of: it was the throne room of Esgallien, and the Witch-queen ruled here, as she did in all the realm, only in this place her whims were played out as soon as they came to mind. There was no delay as messengers whipped their horses for speed to deliver her latest orders, though here there were still whips – knotted and cruel, and other implements of torture. He had seen, and felt, them all.

The greatest of the tortures though was to see and hear through the windows, for the outside world offered hope. But this was a lie born of wishful thinking; his only true hope lay in death.

Each day a prisoner was slain: one that had suffered and passed beyond the threshold of endurance; one no longer capable of begging for mercy. And they *did* beg while they could, not that they had any expectation of receiving it when none that had gone before had.

Yet still the slain spoke with their last breaths. He watched now as an old man, though perhaps he was in fact young, it was hard to tell, recoiled from Ebona's touch.

142

Two guards, one stony faced, the other watching eagerly, held him by the chains remaining on his arms near the base of her throne. Ebona was gracious as always, and her bare feet made no noise as she rose and paced toward him.

The prisoner watched, trembling, fearful, but unable to take his eyes off her.

She came. Reaching out, she caressed his cheeks, and then pressed the palms of her hand against his temples, gazing like a lover into his eyes. He trembled. A moment later he stilled as some force of witchery caught his body. Blood began to seep from his ears. Several bright drops splashed over the polished timber floor.

Then the screaming began. Yet still the man could not move. If he were able, he would have thrashed and kicked and punched. But Ebona held him by the power that was in her, and by that same power she burned his eyes. They sizzled and bubbled in their sockets. Smoke curled from them. A foul stench crept through the room.

A final wisp of flame flickered within the darkened sockets, and then Ebona leaned forward, her face intense.

"Tell me what you see," she said.

Brinhain was sick of this. He had watched the same thing too many times. But he could not look away. That was not permitted, and he had learned that disobedience had a price. What happened now was part of his punishment: to watch others endure torment and thereby observe and anticipate his own fate on a day yet to come. He would rather die by the sword, but that mercy would not be granted to him.

Yet torment was only one of the Witch-queen's purposes. As he watched, the old man spoke in a ragged voice. For though his eyes were gone, as with all her previous victims, by her dark arts she induced in him a vision of some far off place, and he told of what he saw.

"Many horses," he gasped. "Many riders speed to the north, and a white light shimmers about them. A Raithlin leads. He carries a great sword. Bright is its blade."

The man groaned. Fresh blood dribbled from his ears. The old blood dried and darkened on the floor.

"Speak!" Ebona commanded.

"The faces of the riders shine ... but a great darkness gathers behind them. I see mountains. Grim. Tall. Dark. Ash and death shroud them. Rivers run from them, but not of water. Elugs and strange men stream by the tens of thousands. They are a great army, and like a flood they sweep across Galenthern. They come! They come! They come!"

The old man suddenly thrashed. Whatever force held him was no longer of sufficient strength, or perhaps he was so close to death that it no longer had power over him. Only a moment he lashed out, and then he sighed and was gone.

Ebona released his limp body. It fell to the floor, but the Royal Guards hauled on the chains and dragged him away.

The witch's cold eyes turned to King Murhain, watching from his throne.

"See," she said. "The south comes – as I thought they would."

She seemed to Brinhain to look neither happy nor displeased. He wondered why. Perhaps the old legends spoke truly: she fed off death. He would believe anything of her.

But for all her poise, the king seemed restless. There was some struggle going on there, some last flicker of his will that vied to free him from bondage.

"Guards!" he called. "Guards!"

144

Several came. There was an endless procession of them these days, though Brinhain recognized few of them.

"Ready the army," he said. "Send troops to Esgallien Ford. And somebody bring me my sword!"

He made to stand, but Ebona smiled sweetly at him and made a gesture with her hand. A moment longer the king struggled, but the weight of her will prevailed. His face went vacant again, and he collapsed onto the throne.

The guards paid him no heed. They looked to Ebona, and one kneeled before her.

"My Queen. What is your will?"

Ebona gazed at him. "Such a well-mannered boy. But what do I want done? Why, nothing. Nothing at all. Let the southerners come. I have a use for them."

A fell light shone in her eyes, and there was a gleam there that Brinhain had seen before. He had once thought it glee, but now he understood better: it was madness. And it was growing.

She softly stroked her left arm, reaching to her neck and then running her fingers through her unbound hair. She sighed heavily and gave no further answer to the guard.

The man hesitated, then stood and backed away before leaving with the others.

Ebona cast her gaze over the prisoners chained to the wall, and then it settled on him. Brinhain felt the heat of her stare.

She smiled. Her teeth were dazzling white, and she moistened her plump lips.

"Oh, what fun I'm having today." She tilted her head and looked at him like a coy young girl. "Why so sad, sweetling? Don't worry – I haven't forgotten you. Your day of fun is coming."

She laughed softly to herself, a deep thrum in her chest that was almost a purr.

Brinhain looked away. He knew he would die in this room, as would all the others – even the king at the last, and that their passings would be painful. He regretted the things that he had done, regretted serving her. He had chosen the wrong side. And yet he would have died regardless.

Lanrik and the lòhrens were dead themselves, even if they did not realize it. No force in Alithoras could resist the Witch-queen. Not for long anyway. Her appetite was vast, and growing, and even spilling all the blood of the land would not quench her thirst for power.

Perhaps, Brinhain thought, in the very early days when they first met, he could have killed her. But he did not want to then, and it was too late now. He had seen firsthand that she was beyond any keen-edged blade or sharp-pointed weapon, and he did not doubt that likewise, she was beyond any power of lòhrengai.

18. One Small Group

Lanrik turned his gaze to Aranloth.

The lòhren stood, tall and grim, atop the tor. Erlissa and the Lindrath were with them, and one other that they had found waiting for them. The Raithlin camped far below within the shelter of some straggly trees.

A strange mood settled over the small group while they looked out from the height of the hill, but it showed most strongly on Aranloth.

"It comes," he said.

The early morning light shot his white hair through with gold, and his voice throbbed with that eerie tone, that near-chanting cadence that Lanrik associated with foretelling.

"It comes. War. Red war. The battle that long we have striven to avoid."

"What of Esgallien?" the Lindrath murmured. "What do you see?"

Aranloth faced slowly to the north. He closed his eyes, but he gave no immediate answer.

"Smoke and turmoil," he said at length. "Strife and blood."

Lanrik could see nothing out of the ordinary, to either south or north, but the lòhren gazed with a sight beyond that of eyes alone.

An odd feeling settled over Lanrik. He had been through this before. A marauding horde approached from the south, and all that he loved was with him on the tor, or north of it. And everything was imperiled. But this time, it was not quite the same – he was not alone.

Others were with him, even some that were unexpected. The lòhren Aratar was one of them, and he spoke now.

"Have I done right, Careth Tar?"

Lanrik waited for an answer himself. He felt that fate was speeding up and overtaking events, but what Aranloth thought he did not know.

"Should I have brought the sword?" Aratar pressed when he did not get an immediate response. "The dream of the Guardian said that I must, but she did not say why. At first, it seemed proper to act on her advice, but with every league that we traveled south, the greater my doubt grew."

Aranloth glanced at the shazrahad sword, sheathed and held uncertainly in Aratar's old hands. His expression was bleak, almost one of dread.

"Have you done wrong? My mind says yes, but my heart says no. The day will soon come when we find out which of the two is wiser. For your part, I don't see that you had any choice. Guardians do not interfere with the lands outside of their realms. For Carnona to do so is extraordinary. Even I, oldest of the lòhrens, am but a child to her, for her memory and wisdom stretch back to a time before even the Letharn raised their first huts out of grass and banded together in small groups to hunt. I will not question her motives, or guess at what secret knowledge she possesses."

Lanrik considered the lòhren's words. It was an answer that gave no answer. Not that he blamed him for that. Who knew what the sword would bring? Even Conhain had been elusive. It was both blessing and curse, he had said. That was a statement no clearer than Aranloth's. It seemed that lòhrens and the dead both spoke in riddles.

He knew this much though. Blessings were vague; they were something that *might* take shape in the future.

The curse side of things was more definite. It spoke of the destruction of Esgallien, and with such a vast army approaching to bring that about, he had no intention at all of touching the blade that embodied a prophecy of doom.

Aranloth sat down and leaned his back against a boulder. Lanrik noted that it was the very same one that he had once clambered up to look out and watch the approach of the previous southern army. It seemed a lifetime ago now.

"It's time for a council," the lòhren said. "Here we must make our plans, such as we can. Let each of us speak, and may our foresight be as keen as our vision from this tor."

They sat down in a close circle. The sun was warming, but still the cool night air lingered, and a sharp breeze blew from the east.

"It seems to me," Aranloth started, "that our first task must be to overthrow Ebona. Nothing can happen unless that is done first."

The Lindrath nodded agreement. "She must go, and though I hold my own special hatred of her for all that she has done to the Raithlin, still would I say so if she had left us alone. She is the head of the snake, and it is no good trying to cut off the tail while fang and venom remain free to bite and poison."

Aranloth waited, but no one else spoke. "On this matter there seems no dispute," he said. "The question we must answer is how can we do it?"

"I have contacts," the Lindrath said. "There is huge resentment in the city. Only the Royal Guard is corrupted, and perhaps not even all of them. The army, and many men besides, would take up arms against the Witch-queen if they saw hope of victory. I could spread word among them, bring them to a point where they would rise in unison. In the past, Ebona stamped out pockets of rebellion before it had a chance to spread wide."

"What you say is no doubt true," Aratar replied. "But this also is true. If you spur a rebellion against her, a battle must be fought. And she has many servants, as well as her own great and growing power. In such a conflict there would be grave risk that those who rebelled would lose heart in the face of hard odds. And if they did not, then very many would die. Perhaps even thousands, and these are the very same men that we would want to fight the southern army. We could win one war, and in doing so, ruin our chances in the next."

"That may be," the Lindrath said. "And yet how else can we defeat her? In what way can a battle be won without a fight?"

Aranloth stroked his chin. "I see the truth of each point of view. But consider this also. There would not be just one fight – there would be two. On one hand men would fight men. But on the other, Ebona is a force of her own. She has great power, and civil war would feed it. And while it lasted, and at the least it would take several days and spend the lives of many men, she would grow. Already she may be beyond the power of the three lòhrens among us to stymie her. For all these reasons, any sort of military action is likely to fail. It must be the last resort, the choice when all other choices have run dry."

Lanrik knew where this was headed, and he agreed.

"If military action is the last resort," he said, "then what can be tried first? All that is left is some desperate plan that relies on stealth and speed, and only a few people to carry it out."

"To carry out what, exactly?" the Lindrath asked.

150

Lanrik saw by the grim look on his face that he guessed the answer already.

"To bring Ebona to bay, by herself, alone and undefended. And by the power that we possess, if it is enough, to kill her or subdue her and make her a prisoner."

Erlissa spoke for the first time. "I think it would prove impossible to take her prisoner. Her power must now be very great. Even if we did so, who would guard her? Who is incorruptible? For few men can withstand her. Within days she would command the guards that ringed her as though they were her own."

"Then she must be killed," the Lindrath said flatly. "For myself, I think she deserves it. But even so, I'm not proud of the idea. The taking of a life, except for self-preservation, is wrong."

Erlissa looked at him directly. "Yes, but I think it *is* now a matter of self-preservation. The southern army is coming. She will grow strong off all the blood to be spilled. I've seen her like that, and there is a madness within her. She would destroy Esgallien, and the enemy at the same time, and rise as a goddess on a mountain of corpses."

"That is so," Aranloth said. "And after that all Alithoras might fall to her. She must be stopped, and the only way to do that is to kill her, or what passes for death to a creature born of ùhrengai."

"Then our course is set," Lanrik said.

"It is," answered the Lindrath. "But not the exact means by which the attempt will be made."

Aranloth ran a hand through his hair. "That remains in doubt, and in truth, I don't think we can plan for it now. We must first reach Esgallien and see how things stand. But this much is not in doubt. The shazrahad sword was brought for a reason. The Guardian does not

151

interfere in the affairs of men. It is here for a purpose, even if we cannot foresee it. I will take that as a sign, a greater sign than any of our arguments, that our aim is right. This small group here must enter the city and face Ebona. No more plans can we make than that."

The lòhren turned to Aratar. "Will you bear the sword, and guard it, until that time?"

"Yes, Careth Tar. I'll do so. But how shall I know when to relinquish it, and to whom?"

Aranloth gave a sigh. "I do not know, but I feel that when the time comes to hand it to another you will know beyond any doubt."

"Yet whatever our own plans or fortunes," the Lindrath said, "the people of Esgallien must still learn that an army marches against them, lest we fail."

"If we fail," Aranloth said, "then I think the warning will make small difference. And yet you are right."

"Then the Raithlin that are with us should go through the city," the Lindrath said. "Let them spread the word, and if we fail, at least then there is a chance the people will rise against Ebona, throw her off and then defend the realm against the southerners."

Aranloth nodded, but did not answer. No one else spoke and the council ended.

The others left, but Lanrik lingered on the tor by himself for a few moments. There was only him, the windswept top of the hill, and the cairn of Lathmai.

He looked at it, and felt tears in his eyes. He had not forgotten her – would never forget her. Now events, begun in this very place long ago, drew toward a conclusion. He wanted to make a promise to her that he would save Esgallien, just as she had done, but in truth he could make no such vow. This much he knew though: he would try his hardest, even at the cost of his life, just as she had.

He walked by himself down the tor. The hum of insects filled the air, but he heard no sound of those who had descended before him, nor of the bulk of the Raithlin who waited at the bottom. Arliss and Feldring were there, Aratar having brought them, and that gave him joy and hope.

Nevertheless, he had an idea that it was a time of endings. He did not think he would ever see Lathmai's cairn again. He gave a silent farewell, but he also knew that whether he came here again or not, no enemy would tread this ground. He had given the southerners a reason to dread the place, and there was another feel to it as well, comforting to him, but a fear to them. It seemed to him that her spirit lingered here and protected it. He felt her presence, and they would too. They would shun the tor, but that would not stop them from coming to Esgallien.

19. Marked for Death

Several days of hard riding brought Lanrik and the others to Esgallien Ford. There they halted.

"Do you see anything?" Erlissa asked.

"Nothing," Lanrik replied. "The guard here isn't as vigilant since the Raithlin left, but there's always been somebody. I expect we'll see lookouts when we reach the other side."

The Lindrath shifted in his saddle. "Do we really want to attempt a crossing in daylight? There's bound to be trouble."

"Need brooks no delay," Aranloth said. "I won't wait to try and sneak over tonight. Leave the guards to me."

Lanrik did not much like the idea, but he trusted that Aranloth knew what he was doing.

They crossed the stretch of rough ground before the ford. As always, the bend in the river cast up a great deal of debris onto the shore. The horses picked their way between tangles of sun-bleached branches, logs and piles of dried riverweed. The place had a desolate feel, at lest until they reached the water.

The horses moved into it swiftly. Their hooves splashed and clattered, and the river soon ran above their hocks. A man could walk through here easily, but it became much harder near the center where the current was strong and the water rose to waist height. The horses, however, surged ahead and made light work of it.

Lanrik felt vulnerable to attack as they crossed. He kept a close watch on the far bank, but still saw nothing even though it drew quickly closer.

The rush and gurgle of water was loud in his ears. The horses slowed when they reached the halfway point, but still made good progress. He got a feel for what it would be like to an invading army: fear would grip them here, for they could do little but struggle onward, and yet from this point a hail of swift-flighted arrows and long-bladed spears would fall thickly upon them. To misstep was to risk drowning. To go forward was to face the concerted efforts of an enemy bent on your destruction. To go back was the only safe option, but shazrahad commanders often had those who first retreated put to a cruel death as an example to the rest of the army. To try to take the crossing was a grim task. It would be hard, but the coming southern army was vast, and who knew what defense, if any, would stand in its way?

They neared the far bank. The horses surged out of the river, streaming water, and scrambled up the steep slope. Before them lay the realm of Esgallien.

They paused. With the Raithlin, they were a force to be reckoned with, but still Lanrik feared whatever guard was set here. And guard there was.

A cavalry troop blocked their path. There were a hundred men waiting silently on well-trained mounts. They were not Royal Guards, but part of the regular army, and they had the look of experienced soldiers. Lanrik guessed these men were handpicked for the task, and he had to reassess the idea that Ebona did not intend to properly guard the ford.

Their commander urged his mount forward, but only a few paces. He stayed within the protection of his men, all armed with short cavalry bows, arrows fitted to their strings.

"Who are you, and why do you seek entry into Esgallien?"

Aranloth answered. "We're friends of Esgallien, and we come with grave tidings and help."

The commander studied him closely. "Esgallien has few friends in these troubled times. And none of them dwells south of the river. Our orders are to shoot and kill any who attempt to cross. Wherefore should we spare your lives?"

Aranloth laughed. It seemed a strange reaction to the situation.

"You have answered your own question," he said. "Your orders are to kill, yet that you have not done. It's not your way, nor the way of most who dwell in Esgallien."

The commander hesitated, but not for long. "That may be so, yet it is death to disobey orders – so speak quickly or ours may yet be carried out."

"You name her not, but I know whence those orders come. And though you have not said as much, you already know me. Who else would I be, an old man, white-robed and carrying a staff? Long have I come to this land, and until recently, I have always received a good welcome." The lòhren spread his arms in a wide gesture. "With me are the Lindrath, Lanrik and Erlissa, as well as many Raithlin. These you know also."

The commander did not hesitate this time. "I asked for a reason to spare your lives. Instead, you give me a list, as it seems, of everyone in the kingdom with a price on their head. It's a strange way of seeking safety."

Aranloth shrugged. "And yet still you have not shot. Shall I tell you why?"

The commander made no answer, and Aranloth continued. "For many of us you have respect. You knew us before I spoke. You do not believe us traitors, irrespective of your orders, for you know us all as friends. Thus do you forestall your orders, even though it is death to do so."

The commander drew a long breath. "That may all be a near guess. Yet, as you say, it's still death for us to let you pass."

"And yet you will."

"Why are you so sure, old man?"

"I know people. Sometimes, I know them better than they know themselves. And I know this also. You were sent here for a reason. You know the Royal Guards are in favor. You know being posted here is the lowest job in the army, away from the city, away from family and friends. And you know also that there are too few of you to survive should a real enemy strike at Esgallien Ford."

"What of it?"

"Simply this. You say your lives are forfeit if you let us pass. I say this instead. Your lives are *already* forfeit, at least to the Witch-queen. She has abandoned you to death. She will know by now that an enemy comes behind us. The might of the south is raised and war marches toward you. Ebona has no intention of stopping them at the ford, and you, the least liked of her servants, are the most expendable. That is why you are here."

Aranloth paused to let his words sink in. The commander made no move, showing nothing of his emotions. Nevertheless, many men behind him became restless.

"Behold!" Aranloth cried in a suddenly loud voice. "I shall lay bare her treachery."

He lifted high his staff. A silver light shimmered in the air all about them. It showed a net of webs, thin as a spider's castings, though each strand gleamed a wicked red. One pierced the heart of each soldier, and they all led back along a single line that shot toward Esgallien.

"What is it?" The commander asked. And though his face was pale, no tremor of fear was in his voice.

"Think!" Aranloth said. "Think of the old legends of Ebona. Think of that long ago battle that was fought near these very fords, where Conhain fell. Once upon a time all the citizens of Esgallien could tell that story. Is it so swiftly forgotten under the rule of a dark queen?"

The commander gazed back at him steadily. "She would feed of our death."

"Yes."

"Can you free us?"

"No. Not yet. Make no mistake, the same net of witchery is cast over every person in the city. To free everyone, Ebona must die. And that is now our purpose." Aranloth paused a moment before he continued. "Now you know our secret mission. Will you let us pass, or will you follow her orders?"

There was silence after this revelation. Lanrik held his breath. He felt a great still pass over all the Raithlin behind him. They did not move lest they trigger a reaction from the soldiers, yet at a flicker of aggression they would be ready to respond.

The commander made a slight gesture with his hand. At the movement his men lowered their bows and sheathed their arrows.

"You shall pass," he said. "And may luck go with you."

Aranloth nodded. "We shall need it. And luck go with you also. Remember this, should the enemy arrive before reinforcements come, do not throw your lives away. You will likely try to hold the fords, but once a passage is forced, and it will be swiftly if no help arrives, retreat. Do not give up hope of living through this, though you are already marked for death. And if you can spare a man, send him to spread word to those who dwell in the villas outside the wall. In that way many lives and other treasures may be preserved."

The commander saluted him. "It shall be as you say."

Aranloth turned to the Raithlin. "Now we ride, for the enemy comes and doom follows. Ride, if you love Esgallien!"

His roan sprang forward and the others followed. Like swift lightning and the crack of thunder they sped along the road and shot toward the city.

20. The Strange Company

Swift the horses raced, and swift the travelers rode. Naught hindered them, and they let nothing slow them down. The day passed into oblivion in the west, and night grew about them. It was cold and dark, for clouds piled on towering clouds in the east. But no rain fell.

The next day, tired and grim, they came early to the great wall that surrounded Esgallien. River Gate stood before them. The Raithlin had put away their cloaks, though the morning's chill bit them. No word of their coming could yet have reached Ebona, unless by witchery. They knew not what to expect, but they were ready nonetheless.

The gate was closed. They saw nobody, though the usual noises of the city came over the walls and through the gate's arm-thick bars, amplified by the killing tunnel in the wall behind it.

Lanrik shifted uneasily in his saddle and turned to Aranloth.

"Do you think there'll be Royal Guards here, or ordinary soldiers?"

The lòhren kept looking ahead. "We were lucky at the ford. I wouldn't count on that again."

As if to prove his words they now saw movement. A score of men walked through the tunnel, having descended from one of the two towers that guarded the gate.

Lanrik's heart sank. They were Royal Guards. What was more, it did not take twenty men to open the gate. So many meant one thing alone: the travelers were recognized. It was not unexpected. They knew there was little chance of entering the city unnoticed. But they had not foreseen that the gate would be closed during daylight hours.

Their captain drew his sword. His men followed suit. Their blades, long and sharp, crafted of the highest Esgallien skill, glimmered within the dark of the tunnel.

The Raithlin drew their own swords. Lanrik found his own come readily to hand, and the three staffs of the lòhrens were held high. Yet no word was uttered.

It seemed that the captain would speak, but even as he opened his mouth, he paused. The men behind him faltered also. For what reason, Lanrik did not know. The guards paled. Their faces shone white in the black tunnel and strength seemed to drain from their limbs. Their arms lowered, and several blades dropped from limp-fingered hands to clang on the cobbled road.

Lanrik wondered if the lòhrens had worked some magic, some feat to achieve this. If so, it was the first time that he had ever seen them use their powers against men, rather than a sorcerous enemy. He looked to their faces, but they seemed as surprised as he was.

He glanced back at the Royal Guards. There was fear in their expressions, and some other emotion that he could not name. His skin prickled at the eeriness of it all.

He noticed that the guards did not look at him, nor the lòhrens. Rather, they directed their wide-eyed gaze at something further back.

He turned to look. As he did so, he noticed the lòhrens do the same.

His heart gave a sudden leap. Royal Guards, lòhrens and Raithlin were all forgotten. Something else held his attention and made his tongue cleave to the roof of his mouth.

Conhain was there. The great king, mounted on his massive warhorse. No sword was by his side, nor any scabbard. Lanrik was suddenly aware of the weight of the blade in his own hand. And though the king was weaponless, the glint of battle was in his eyes. His horse snorted impatiently.

The east wind blew, cold and chill, and it ruffled Conhain's ghostly hair. His horse shook its head and the light all about it shimmered.

Aranloth stiffened. "So much for plans," he whispered to Lanrik. "Our destiny is to ride in the open, rather than to use stealth. The final confrontation comes sooner than expected."

The lòhren turned to the front. Straight he sat on his horse. His white robes flowed and glimmered about him. He spoke loudly to the Royal Guards.

"Open the gate!" he commanded. "Your king is come to the city!"

For a moment they stood in dismay. Many trembled in fear, and then some bowed while others fled. The captain drew himself up. He looked as though he would defy Aranloth, and then he sagged. Without taking his eyes off Conhain, the man loosed the great bars that held the gate in place and then swung it open. After that, he kneeled and bowed his head. The men left with him did likewise.

Slowly the travelers rode through the way opened to them. No one spoke. The only sound was the clatter of hooves on the cobbles. It echoed back from the confines of the dark tunnel.

They paused as they came out from beneath the shadow of Esgallien's wall. Sunlight fell upon them again. They were inside the city and upon the Hainer Lon; the Heroes Way as men called it.

Aranloth addressed the Raithlin. "Stealth will no longer serve us. Now, we have a surer road to the palace, though not a safer one. Put on your cloaks. Wear them with pride, for you have earned it. We will all ride now to the palace. And the king, I deem, will come with us."

Lanrik drew his cloak from the saddlebag and put it on. It felt good. It had been long since he openly declared who he was in this city.

Already eyes were on them, for those citizens going about their ordinary business had stopped to watch. Awe held them in its grip, for they saw Conhain. None could fail to recognize him, and none failed to see the ghostly shimmer of light that fell from him and his otherworldly horse like a mist of water from a fountain.

Aranloth urged his roan forward. The others followed. They moved in a solemn procession along the Hainer Lon.

Lanrik looked back as they rode. Many in the crowd followed them. He saw something else, also. One of the Raithlin drew an object from her saddlebag. It was not her cloak, which she already wore. It was the twisted talnak horn that long ago he had given to the Lindrath after freeing Erlissa from the shazrahad's tent.

The beaten gold encasing the horn's mouth glimmered. The two gold bands about it shimmered, and the scrimshaw carved upon its polished surface flickered and twisted like a live thing in the shifting light.

The Lindrath took it. A moment he held it tentatively, and then with sudden conviction he raised it to his lips. The horn sang a long and winding note. It was a challenge that filled the city streets and ran far ahead. But it was more than a challenge. It was also a call to arms. Before the last echoes died off, men and women who had been watching from the side streets joined the growing procession.

Thus did they progress through the city. At whiles the Lindrath blew the horn, and the crowd behind them ever increased. A multitude was now before them also, but it parted and let the company through, and then joined the throng after the riders passed.

So they continued along the Hainer Lon and passed by the great places of the city. The crowd behind them was at first hushed, but after a while some began to sing. They murmured softly in the beginning, snatches of old songs here and there, and then a few voices rose up high and clear and sweet. They settled on an old ballad that recounted the deeds of Conhain, and this the whole crowd soon took up until it boomed in slow majesty throughout the city. At first it was hundreds of voices, and then the deep-throated song of thousands rumbled like majestic thunder and the very ground shook.

Lanrik rode on. No one about him spoke. If he glanced back he saw the awed faces of the Raithlin and behind them again the mighty figure of Conhain. The king gazed straight ahead. He did not speak, nor did he make any sign. But he rode tall and proud, and his otherworldly eyes glinted.

What aid a spirit could give, Lanrik did not know. And yet the die was cast. Doom approached and the final confrontation with Ebona neared. He did not know what would happen, but no single person in the city would be the same hereafter.

At times the singing slowed as they passed one of the beloved places of the city such as the Merenloth. Then the crowd would cry in one voice: "Conhain! Conhain! The king is come again!"

At length they came to Conhain Court, and thence to the gate before the palace grounds. The corpse that was hung there long ago still remained, though now it was a thing of leathered skin and bleached bones held together

164

by ragged cloth. There were no guards. They had fled before the procession arrived.

The riders paused, and the crowd, filling Esgallien's great court, fell silent.

The Lindrath looked strange. Slowly he dismounted and undid the chains that held the corpse. With great reverence he gathered the remains in the Raithlin cloak the man had once worn with pride, though now it was a tattered thing, stained by gore and shredded by the sharp beaks of carrion crows. Yet still the Raithlin motif of the trotting fox looking back over its shoulder stood out clearly.

The Lindrath laid his burden down to the side of the gate. There he stood a moment, head bowed. When he spoke, his voice was deep and strong, and it carried back into the crowd:

> *Our duty is to serve and protect*
> *Our honor is to fight but not hate*
> *Our love is for all that is good in the world*

From the mouths of all the Raithlin came a reply:

> *Well did you serve and protect*
> *High was your honor, low was your hate*
> *Your love for good was a beacon of light*

The crowd spoke no word, but from somewhere within it the wailing of a single woman rose in heartbreak.

The Lindrath raised his head. He moved to the gate and tested it. The rattle of metal bars and hinges was loud, but it did not budge.

"The gate is locked," he said.

Aranloth nudged his roan forward. "Stand aside," he ordered.

The lòhren leaned forward in the saddle and placed the tip of his staff against the wrought iron lock. Nothing happened at first, and then suddenly the whole gate trembled. With a loud crack, a high-pitched scream of tortured metal, and finally a puff of black smoke, the lock shattered.

The gate swung open with a crash, and the Lindrath remounted. They all rode through in silence and entered the royal gardens. They followed the Hainer Lon as it led to the palace. The crowd flowed behind them like a sea spilled onto dry ground from the basin that long hemmed it.

There were no guards. The travelers saw nobody before them, either in the grounds or at windows or balconies.

They came to the palace doors, great things of ancient oak, nearly as old as the city. They were shut.

Silence hung over everything like a shroud. No word or even whisper could be heard.

Lanrik gazed at the palace, seeking signs of the enemy. He saw nothing, but he knew that Ebona would have learned of their coming. And she would not have fled. She was inside, though what she would do now, he could not guess. He wondered what they should do in their own turn, but the blank walls and vacant windows offered no answer.

21. Nothing Lasts Forever...

Into the silence the Lindrath blew the talnak horn. It was loud but remote, a clear and high series of winding notes that reverberated with otherworldly grace.

When the last echo died, Aranloth cried out. His steel-edged voice carried far, no doubt penetrating deep into the palace.

"Ebona! You are no queen of Esgallien. Leave your stolen throne! Come hither, before the people of the realm and receive judgment at the hand of a true king!"

There was silence again. It lay over the city like a deep shadow, but one filled with fear. For none had heard the Witch-queen addressed so before, and all feared her fury at such an affront.

The crowd shuffled back. As they moved, a low moan rippled through them.

And then Ebona came. Aranloth's challenge could not be denied. At first her coming was little more than a faraway rumor. There was a tremor in the earth as though of great powers stirring. Lights flashed in windows. Glass cracked and then shattered.

At length, the great doors of the palace blasted open in a furious ruin of splintered timber.

Ebona stood in the wreckage. Not as a ruler of Esgallien, but as Queen of the World. A breeze fanned her unbound hair. It blazed golden as the sun. Her white dress dazzled. And her eyes, eyes that shimmered one moment green and the next blue, gazed at them with the keenness of flashing swords.

She cast a contemptuous glance at Aranloth and the Raithlin, but when her gaze rested on Conhain it showed a flicker of doubt.

With a shake of her head she turned back to Aranloth and laughed as a mother does at a child attempting some deed, and though failing at it, refusing to give up.

"You think to defeat me, old man? I am Ebona, and I am become a god. No power can resist me. No nation shall not fall under my sway. If all the lòhrens who ever lived raised a hand against me now, still could I brush them aside. If I wish a land to rule, I shall take it for my own. If I seek slaves to serve me, then even the proud Halathrin shall bow at my feet and ask my will. But to you, old man, I will not give the choice of servitude. Once you caused me pain. I remember it still. But I am stronger now. Strong. Strong as the bones of the world! And I shall pay you back, like for like, a thousand fold."

Ebona lifted her pale arms. The earth trembled. Water gushed from the ground. Great rents appeared, and from the fissures rose the noise of stone grinding on stone.

"Will you contend with me, old man? Or will you bow before me and beg for mercy?"

She bent her gaze upon him. He stood, leaning on his staff, and he seemed the old man that she named him. Nothing so frail could stand in the face of her onslaught, and it appeared that he would drop to his knees. A moment he trembled. A moment Lanrik held his breath. The silver diadem on his brow gleamed. His hands held tight the staff, and then he straightened. He raised his bowed head and lifted the staff before him.

"You are not a god," he said calmly. "Nor are your plans ripe. And when they do ripen, if that should come to pass, you will find the fruit of your labor is rotten. Madness will devour you, if it has not already."

168

He looked at her from his old eyes, and there was sadness in them. But not fear.

"Pull back from the brink," he said, "and live. Continue, and you will die."

The Witch-queen stared at him, and then she laughed softly.

"Threats? Threats from the great and wise Aranloth? But you cannot threaten me. You are as nothing, and these others are less than nothing. And the ghost of Conhain is lesser still. I killed him once, and I enjoyed the deed. What is left is nothing more than the glimmer of light from the life that I snuffed out long ago. I could send him to the great dark, there to wail in eternity with the twitch of my finger."

Lanrik noted that for all her words she did no such thing. Nor did she attack any of the others. She was stalling, buying time for a hidden purpose.

"Why do you wait, Ebona?" he said. "Have you summoned guards from all over the city to slaughter the innocent behind us? Would you feed and grow on their death as you have on others before them?"

Ebona's gaze pinned him as though by the weight of a suddenly felled tree. He could not breathe. It seemed that his heart stilled. He reached for the hilt of his sword, but his hand fumbled.

"You!" Ebona said. "You could have been a great king. Better than the dross of Esgallien that I have suffered to sit beside me this last little while." She paused, and when she continued, her voice was softer. "Perhaps you still could be. Come to me. Come to me now, and maybe I shall forgive your trespasses against me."

She beckoned him with her hand. Lanrik felt a wave of dizziness. It was all he could do to stay on his feet. Without at first realizing it, he took a slow step toward her. His foot moved again, taking a second step that he did not wish, and yet some will other than his own commanded him. A third and fourth step followed more promptly.

Ebona looked at him. Her expression was almost kindly. "You are mine now, boy."

Lanrik gathered the tattered remnants of his own will. His fumbling hand found the hilt of his sword and swiftly he drew it lest the power to command his own body be lost again.

A cold thrill ran through him. He remembered the courage of Conhain and it gave him hope. At the same moment he felt the full force of Ebona's will, redoubled upon him. Pain shot through his arm, and then it grew numb as though blood ceased to flow through it. Yet still he had strength, and free will. And he used both.

Swift he struck. The great blade glittered. In one motion he sprang forward, and the sharp edge cut through the air. It struck the Witch-queen and sliced a wide arc through her flesh.

Red blood flowed and gushed. She staggered back, surprised that someone could defy her will, and she cried out with unexpected pain. Crimson stains covered her white dress. Bright blood spattered over the tiles beneath her bare feet.

She screamed. It was a sound that began with anguish but it ended in wrath. He fell to his knees, the effort to defy her had wearied him to the point of fainting, but she did not fall. She now stood tall and straight. The blood ceased to flow. It burned and sizzled until a haze of smoke swirled through the air, and then when that blew away she was revealed just as she was earlier. No stain marred the white of her dress; and no wound pained her, unless in memory.

"You will pay for that, boy," she hissed. "Did you not know that no sword can kill me? Not even a Halathrin trinket? I am invulnerable to steel, even as I am warded against ùhrengai, elùgai, and lòhrengai. That is what it means to be a god."

Lanrik felt someone approach from behind. A shimmering light spilled over him. It was Conhain.

"Witch," said the king. "You speak the truth. But not *all* the truth. To these powers you are immune. But you are no god, nor shall ever be. Neither will you have thralls, either lesser or greater. It would have been well for you to listen to the counsels of Aranloth, but as of old, you set his wisdom to naught and raise your own too high."

He held now in his hand the shazrahad sword and raised it slowly. Lanrik had not seen Aratar give it to him, and he wondered at the lòhren's strange choice to surrender it to a spirit without body and little more than light for form. Even as the king gripped it Lanrik saw the wrapped leather hilt through his shimmering hand.

Conhain stepped forward and thrust the blade at Ebona. She leaped back, but the point still drove deep into her, though it was not such a blow as Lanrik had dealt.

Ebona straightened. The blade in Conhain's hand flickered, and smoke curled along its edges. Colored lights played and shimmered down its length. A great shadow went over the sun and the world dimmed.

"You, I will kill again," Ebona said with relish.

She stepped forward, but a look of puzzlement crossed her face. Conhain watched her without movement.

The Witch-queen glanced suddenly at the smoking blade in his hand.

"No!" she screamed.

171

Conhain remained still, yet the sword he held now burned with a writhing fire of three strands: white, silver and red.

The earth rumbled. Flames darted inside the fissures of the earth. Ebona raised herself to full height. With one long hand she reached out, claw-like, toward Conhain. But then a white mist rose in a cloud from the earth. It clung to her. It drew her down. She struggled against it, but the mist became one with her, or her one with it, and down her nebulous form seeped into the ground until she was gone and nothing remained but the memory of her fierce gaze.

"The witch is dead," Aranloth said somberly. "Slain by ùhrengai, lòhrengai and elùgai combined." There was no tone of regret in his voice, nor was there one of happiness.

Conhain sighed. He dropped the shazrahad sword, but only the hilt clanged against the tiles. What was left of the blade drifted away as ash on the wind, though it seemed to Lanrik that he saw a figure in that residue: a cloaked and hooded form, but it dispersed before he was sure.

The otherworldly light about the great king dimmed. He turned to Aranloth. No words they spoke, but a look of understanding passed between them. He turned then to Lanrik, his form shimmering and losing whatever substance it had.

"Nothing lasts forever," he whispered. "Not tyranny, nor despair, nor even great evil."

A moment the king looked at him, and then he was gone. The world seemed dark without his light, but then the clouds parted and the sun shone again.

Lanrik turned to the massed crowd of Esgallien. Conhain's sword was in his hand, still blood-wetted.

172

"The Witch-queen is dead," he cried. "But our troubles are not yet over. An army comes from the south. It is a host such as Esgallien has not faced in a thousand years. We must prepare for war!"

A ripple of fear ran through the crowd just when they had embraced sudden joy. Lanrik had no wish to steal it from them, but they must know the truth: their peril was as great now as it ever was.

Had the crowd known of the prophecy embodied by the shazrahad sword, a deadlier fear would have run through it. For now a king of the north had held the blade, spirit though he was, and Lanrik saw the blessing and the curse of that.

Ebona was dead, killed by perhaps the one thing that she had never expected to exist: an artifact of the powers that formed and substanced the world, united as they had never been before or likely ever would again. The Guardian had planned it. Perhaps Aranloth had guessed it. But surely the prophecy must now quicken in response.

War was upon them, and Lanrik had little hope.

22. Who Speaks for Esgallien?

Lanrik gazed from the parapet of the tower. He was weary as he had seldom been before, and there was no hope of respite. Things would only get worse.

River Gate was below him, for he stood on the right hand tower that guarded it, looking out across the well-tended lands that lay between the city and Esgallien Ford. What he saw was peaceful. The grape vines were bare, their crops long since stripped away. The nut trees were stark also, their hoary branches holding few remnants of autumn color. The precious harvest of their many groves was long since gathered and stored within the cellars of the red-roofed and pale-walled villas.

It all looked as it should. But things were not as they seemed. The enemy had marched with near-impossible speed, or else, and Aranloth deemed this far more likely, a different army from the one they had seen on Galenthern had left earlier from the eastern reaches of the Graèglin Dennath, where the elug population was greatest. Either way, it had arrived soon after they had themselves crossed the ford.

Whatever the case, the enemy had come at the same time as Ebona was overthrown. The hundred men who held the ford were tasked with an enemy beyond their strength. Yet still they held their ground for several hours. It was not much, but it was dearly bought by the blood of seventy soldiers. Yet their sacrifice saved countless others, for warning reached the villas and the people dwelling there had an opportunity to flee to the city. But their homes, and most of their goods, and the wine and nuts and other harvest from their grand estates were left behind.

If he looked closely, he saw smoke on the horizon. That was the first sign of the sacking and destruction of the villas and the advance of the enemy. More would follow, and there was no point sending solders to contest the southerner's march. Esgallien's army was too few and too ill-prepared. Moreover, every man saved now was one more to defend the walls later. And that was needful.

Lanrik was no military leader. He had not sought to head the defense, but trust was much diminished in the army, for some of the generals had sided with the Witch-queen. The soldiers only trusted him: he was a Raithlin, he had defied Ebona and he bore Conhain's sword. Thus they served him, yet little could he offer in return save a true heart.

Esgallien's wall would repel the enemy, or it would not. There was little strategy to be had in that, and little difference he could make save to bring the people together to fight as one. But that was no small thing.

Yet he had made one decision that he thought necessary. The generals did not like it. They argued that it would dishearten the soldiers. But the generals did not perceive the strength of the enemy army, nor had they seen the sorcery of an elùgroth. Of these things, they would learn soon. Despite their protests, he had taken the precaution of evacuating Esgallien's population northward. A vast column, protected by what soldiers could be spared, and taking with them the greatest treasures of the city, moved north. From there they could strike out to safety in Camarelon, or Cardoroth, should the city fall.

The generals had forbidden it. Lanrik had ordered it. In the end, Aranloth had lost his temper and called the generals fools. They did not like it, any more than that a Raithlin led instead of one of their own number. But they endured it, for they had little choice, and the counsel of a lòhren carried weight.

He knew in his heart that it was right. And as the smoke spread in the south, he wished the column well. They would need luck, but they should survive. He did not think the city would. Its streets were empty now, except for soldiers and errand riders, but he feared that soon elugs and Azan would swarm the roads and ways that he loved. But this they would never do without contest. He gripped the hilt of Conhain's sword at his side and vowed to make it so. And who knew? He had seen victory against likelihood before. Perhaps it would be so now, prophecy or not.

"They'll reach the city by dark," Aranloth said. "The vanguard at any rate."

The lòhren stood with him on the parapet. His face was grim. The expressions of all the others were the same. Even Arliss seemed subdued. Some of the other Raithlin were nearby atop the city wall, mixed in amongst the army. Most were out scouting. He wished above all else to know how Erlissa fared, but she was down by the gate. It was close by, but she may as well have been a mile distant, for he could not talk to her or even see her.

"If the vanguard is small, we might consider a sortie when it arrives," Lanrik offered.

"Perhaps," Aranloth agreed. But he did not sound convinced, and Lanrik knew why. There would be elùgroths with the army to lead it, as well as shazrahads. They would not err by overreaching themselves in that way.

As the day progressed that thought proved correct. The army came, bringing smoke and fire with it, laying waste to Esgallien's fair fields. But it came slowly, testing out the way with caution. Scouts reported its number at twenty thousand, and that it progressed without a vanguard at all, unless an entire army could be considered such for a greater army that followed.

"The nut groves are burning," Lanrik said. "As are the vines and villas."

"It's the enemy's way," Aranloth answered. "For win or lose, elùgroths would destroy. And they have apt pupils in the elugs. There's nothing there that cannot be rebuilt though, yet some of those nut groves seem old, even to me, and they would take generations of farmers to replant and tend before they bore a harvest as do these. But they will be planted and bear again, one day."

Lanrik did not reply. He knew what the lòhren was doing, and it was right. Every word they said would spread through Esgallien's army. The soldiers must have hope, or there was no point in fighting at all. Hope kept people going. And though he knew this, and acted his part, he had little for himself. At least, not of saving the city. His hope lay in the safety of its people, who escaped further north each hour.

When the sun arced toward the west and the afternoon came, the enemy army drew into view. The haze of smoke and distance no longer hid it, but it remained a dark thing, a mass of shadows and black cloaks, of furtive shapes that seethed forward, eager but wary.

The army approached, and its long shadow marched ever ahead of it. Battle would not be fought today, but tomorrow would be as red a dawn as Lanrik had ever seen.

He stood still and erect, showing no sign of his misgivings. At times he hummed some of the old tunes that the Lindrath had taught him, and at others he joked with Arliss. He set an example to the men, and though he did not disguise the size of the battle ahead of them, he let them know that no army, no odds and no sorcery would dismay him.

The southern army neared the wall as dusk fell. Vast it was; a black thing of serried ranks, proud horsemen, cruel elugs and massive lethrin. And at its head were shazrahads, bearded old men, grim and fierce to look upon. And before even them, seven elùgroths.

"It could be worse," Aranloth said. "Seven is many, but their power would have been the greater with Elù-Randùr."

Lanrik saw that the shadow of anguish was still on the lòhren's face. He gave no answer. Aranloth's words were true, and it was something to be thankful for. Yet there were still seven sorcerers set against but three lòhrens. And what form of attack would their sorcery take?

The enemy host established a camp and fortified their position. Swiftly they dug embankments and threw up an earth wall, which they palisaded with timber spikes. Picket lines were established, of both elugs and horsemen, to guard the perimeter.

Dark fell and many thousands of fires sprang up, fuelled by the closest of the once great nut groves of Esgallien.

Smoke drifted up to the battlements, and then spread as a cloud over the city. It lingered through the long night, and Lanrik retired to his chamber where he slept restlessly when not woken by army messengers or returning scouts.

Dawn came at last. A breeze started to blow the smoke away, but a blood-red sun rose, a signal that set a stage for battle.

The elug war drums began to beat at the first red rays. A great cry went up from the enemy host:

Ashrak ghùl skar! Skee ghùl ashrak!
Skee ghùl ashrak! Ashrak ghùl skar!

The chant flowed without beginning or end. The drums hastened. Stamping boots thundered, and Lanrik felt the dread of the elug chant:

Death and destruction! Blood and death!
Blood and death! Death and destruction!

He took a deep breath, annoyed by the weight of chain mail that he was unused to wearing. The elugs raced toward the wall. Thousands of them, thicker than autumn's leaves on the ground.

The Lindrath blew his horn. As the long notes sounded Lanrik drew Conhain's sword.

"Esgallien!" he cried, giving voice to the battle-cry of the city that had been heard for near on a thousand years, though never yet had it been shouted from the city walls.

The soldiers gave answer. All along the rampart the cry echoed. It released fear. It freed the body for action. The generals said it frightened the enemy, too. Lanrik did not believe that. Not this enemy. Many things were said by those who were supposed to know. Only occasionally were they right.

The elugs streamed to the wall. They carried great ladders, high enough to reach the top of the battlement. They brought also knotted and iron hooked climbing ropes. A thick spray of arrows descended on them. Many of the enemy fell, but the rest came on. In ordered ranks after them approached elug archers. They answered the fire from atop the wall, trying to kill or hinder Esgallien's archers. Yet their arrows fell short. They were not yet in range.

Like a wave of water the elugs hit the wall. Ladders were thrown up. Ropes were cast high. The noise and tumult of their onslaught was loud.

All about Lanrik, and all along the rampart for hundreds of strides to each side of River Gate, men were busy. Archers fired. Spearmen hurled their ash shafts. Heavy stones were dropped. Axes hacked at rope. Many hands seized, pushed and toppled ladders. The elugs perished in great numbers, but still they came.

The enemy archers drew closer. Their barbed arrows now reached the battlements, and a soldier near Lanrik suddenly stiffened and fell back, an arrow in his neck. He lay still in a pool of his own blood. Swiftly men came from behind and stretchered him way, hastening down the tower stairs. A hospital was established in the city, but no healing would help this man. Others soon came and spread sawdust over the blood.

Ahead, an elug clambered over the rampart, swinging up one arm at a time along a rope. He jumped over the top, a dagger clenched between his teeth.

He had no chance to pull it and throw, still less to draw his sword. Lanrik stepped forward and slashed. The elug's head toppled back, falling far below. Blood spurted. A moment later he pushed the thrashing body over too.

A soldier hewed with an axe at the rope and severed it. Lanrik looked down and a half a dozen more elugs fell to their deaths.

A talnak horn sounded. It was not the Lindrath's. It drifted up to them from the enemy camp and the enemy retreated.

Their first attack had failed. Those left alive streamed away, harried by arrows, but their archers redoubled their fire, helping to cover the retreat, and merlons or not in the battlement, some of Esgallien's archers were hit as they fired through the crenels.

A cry leapt to the throats of the soldiers.

"Esgallien! Esgallien! Esgallien!"

Lanrik joined in, but soon a weary quiet settled over both armies. The sun rose higher. Flies swarmed over blood. Crows cawed in the distance.

"It was but a first test," Aranloth said.

"It'll be a long day," the Lindrath answered.

Thus the battle continued in a series of assaults, wave after wave. Some rose higher, and several times fighting broke out on the rampart, but these instances were few and repelled without great loss.

Gore spattered Lanrik. Conhain's sword dripped blood. At whiles when there was a lull in the fighting, Raithlin scouts brought news: the southern army continued to swell. But it sought only the destruction of Esgallien and sent no troops to harry Esgallien's fleeing population.

"So far, so good," Lanrik said to Aranloth after speaking with the last scout. "The people are well on their way, and the enemy either doesn't know or doesn't care."

"They don't know," Aranloth said. "And let's hope it stays that way a little longer. If they did, they would have sent off Azan to pursue. Their cavalry does them no good here, and they've more than enough men to spare."

They spoke no more. The soldiers around them grew tense again, and then a horn blew on the fields far below. Another charge was coming.

The enemy swarmed over the churned ground outside the wall. On they came. Dust rose about them. Cries and curses tore the air. Soon they clambered up the walls and this time many made it to the top.

A great elug leapt through a crenel, followed by a swarm of his smaller brethren. Lanrik charged them. His sword swung and flashed. Bodies toppled. Blood spurted. But then they pressed him back.

Other men leapt to the fray. The fighting was desperate. Lanrik slipped on blood and fell. The great elug sprang through the melee toward him. He held high a curved blade, and then slashed it down. Lanrik rolled. There was a clang as metal struck stone. He jumped to his feet, but the elug attacked too swiftly for him. The scimitar smashed into his own blade, knocking it from his hand with a numbing jar.

Lanrik did the only thing he could. He charged forward, taking the elug in a bear hug. He smelled the other's fetid breath, and his hands slipped as they searched for a grip on the elug's oiled chain mail. But he pressed on and drove his foe back toward the wall.

A while they struggled. Battle surged about them. For the moment, there was no help, and if Lanrik lived or died it would be at his own doing.

The elug dropped his sword, useless to him in this close-quarter wrestle. But he did not forgo weapons altogether. About his wrists were hardened leather bands, pricked with iron spikes, and he managed to scrape one of these against Lanrik's neck.

Lanrik cursed. He felt blood dribble down beneath his mail coat. With a mighty heave he lifted the elug clean off the ground and cast him over the battlement. The spikes ripped as the elug fell. Pain raced through him. But then the elug was gone, screaming into oblivion.

The battle about them suddenly changed. The elugs lost heart. They sought to group together, to survive until another wave of their brethren came to the walls, but such was not their fate.

Lanrik retrieved his blade. When it flashed once more the cry of "Esgallien!" roared to life. The soldiers of the city renewed their efforts, and the enemy was soon slain. Their corpses were cast over the wall whence they came. Beneath the rampart the enemy retreated, swarming back to its fortified camp.

"They'll try something new, next time," Aranloth said.

Lanrik did not answer him. He gasped for breath and squatted down, careless of the blood and gore about him. He needed rest. But the fighting was not done yet.

The shadows lengthened. The day drew nigh to its end. One final assault was made while the sun still hung in the sky.

Lanrik watched, but he felt little fear. He was numb. He had seen more death and pain and destruction than most saw in a lifetime. He would never be able to un-see much of this, and if he lived, he knew some images would trouble him all the days of his life. Yet for now, all he felt was a great weariness, but at the same time a steady, driving, indomitable will – a determination to fight, to not give in, to continue until the last.

But it was not elugs that came against them next. Lethrin strode forward. The drums were stilled. The great creatures moved in silence. Armor they wore, but he knew that their skin and flesh was hard like rock anyway.

A storm of arrows fell upon them. They did not stumble. Spears flew and crashed amid their ranks; they paid no heed. Ladders they carried, sturdy constructions designed to take their great weight, and these they thrust against the walls.

The lethrin climbed. They were not swift like elugs, but dart and spear hindered them not, nor cast rock. The men dislodged some of the ladders, using long poles to do so, but it was slow work and though the lethrin did not climb swiftly, it was fast enough.

Yet Lanrik had met their kind once before, and old legends spoke of them also. And Aranloth had counseled him, so he was not unprepared.

At his signal, men brought vats of oil to the threshold of the wall. These were emptied over the timber of the ladders, and the lethrin also. Archers stepped forward, flaming rags, soaked in the same oil, wrapped around their arrowheads. They let fly the shafts.

Fires burned. They were slow to catch, but they did not go out. A reek rose. The lethrin died in silence. Many toppled, flaming through the air. None retreated. Some few made it to the battlement.

At another signal from Lanrik axmen came forward. They hewed and struck, and the lethrin hammered back with heavy maces. Many men died, but the axes bit where swords would not, and the lethrin began to fall.

Lanrik joined the fray. He had no axe, but found that Conhain's blade, forged of Halathrin steel, cut where all of Esgallien's swords would not. Three lethrin he killed, including the last alive on the battlement.

The soldiers cast the bodies into the reek of smoke and smoldering oil below. Yet no few of their own had also fallen. The stretcher-bearers were busy, and many wounded were taken away with horrific injuries from the great maces.

The sun dropped low in the west, and then sunk below the horizon. In the quiet, an elùgroth came forward. He walked slowly, his hands held high. He did not carry his wych-wood staff.

Lanrik sent word along the lines. *Do not shoot unless he attacks.*

Aranloth stood nearby. "He will not attack. Not tonight. His day will come tomorrow."

The elùgroth came to a halt below the tower, facing River Gate.

"I am Gar-galen," he said, "and I command this army. Who speaks for Esgallien?"

Lanrik answered. "I do."

The elùgroth looked up a moment without answer.

"I do not bandy words with nameless vagabonds," he said at length. "Fetch me your king."

Lanrik grinned. "A vagabond you name me, but your own words give lie to your insult. You know who I am. I have given you cause to do so."

The elùgroth's face darkened. "Just get your king, and I will treat with him."

"You'll treat with me, or you can wait before the wall like a starving dog pawing in vain at a closed gate."

The elùgroth stiffened. "I have killed many for less than that," he said.

Lanrik drew his sword. The great blade of Conhain gleamed with the last dull rays of the dying sun, and his eyes burned fiercely.

"Then come. Come kill me now – if you can. I'm a warrior, but you're a great sorcerer. Come kill me, or speak your piece and go. I have other and better things to do than play word games with the likes of you."

The elùgroth raised his hand. His pallid skin shone palely in the dusk. He hissed, and it was a sound more animal than human.

"Speak!" cried Lanrik. "Or go back whence you came!"

The elùgroth stood very still. "Know this, O Raithlin. Neither swords nor courage nor even lòhrengai will save this city. Tomorrow it will be ours. This choice I give you, and this alone. Open the gate by dawn, surrender all arms, and I shall spare the population. A shazrahad will rule them instead of your king, and they will become one

185

with the mighty south. Defy us, and all will die, to the least and last, and we shall raze your city to dust."

Night fell. The first stars kindled in the sky, and Lanrik gave no immediate answer. Not because he did not have one, but because he knew well enough that no one would be spared, surrender or otherwise. History was proof of that, for other cities had fallen before now and nothing remained of them besides dry names of half-forgotten lore. What he had now was a chance for a little more time, an opportunity for Esgallien's escaping citizens to get further away, for it was clear that the enemy did not yet know of their exodus.

"We shall think on this," he said at length. "At dawn, you will have your answer."

The elùgroth lingered a moment. Hatred marked his face, but he spoke no more. He turned and walked back to the host.

Lanrik looked at Aranloth. "Well, how was that? I hope I did rightly."

Aranloth shook his head. "The elùgroth was not Elù-Randùr, but he's still a sorcerer of great power. Why did you think it wise to antagonize him?"

Lanrik shrugged. "Because he deserved it. But look who's talking. You do it all the time."

Aranloth suddenly grinned. "Well, maybe I do. But that just makes me a bad example to follow. Anyway, to answer your question, I think you did well. You hid from him that neither the Witch-queen nor King Murhain rules anymore, and you bought more time for Esgallien's people. I don't think they'll send out any scouts until tomorrow, if at all."

"Then that's as much as could be hoped for," Lanrik said.

He retired that evening to his small chamber near the top of the tower. There was little in it save a low cot, a table and several chairs.

The cot saw little use. All night he received reports from Raithlin and issued orders. He slept for an hour before dawn, and yet he woke refreshed a little while before the sun rose.

A soldier bought him in a bowl of cold water and a towel. He set about shaving and washing. It seemed the only chance he had for peace and quiet. When he returned to the walls he would get no rest from battle and decisions, and it would be a long day. Perhaps the longest of his life.

The sorcerer's offer had not been considered. Not by him, nor anyone else. No one trusted elùgroths, and for that lack of faith history gave good reason.

He missed Erlissa. He had not seen her in a long time. Yet she was close, being busy at the gate. It was a weak spot, as any gate in a wall of stone must be. She made preparations there with Aratar for defense against sorcery. For surely that is where such an attack would come. If the gate fell, then all the men on the wall would be useless.

At length, he gave a sigh, belted on Conhain's sword and strode up a short flight of stairs to the parapet. He arrived as the eastern sky showed signs of graying and the stars began to fade. Aranloth was already there.

They waited in silence. The sun rose, perhaps the last Esgallien would ever see. Certainly, many men warmed by its light this day would lie cold and unmoving tomorrow.

The elùgroth came forward. Again, he was by himself. But this time he carried his wych-wood staff.

The sorcerer halted and stood waiting. No question he asked, and Lanrik prepared to speak. What he said now would not be for the benefit of the enemy. His words must give heart to the men who fought for their home.

23. A Red Dawn

The taste of ashes was in Lanrik's mouth. The sun hung low in the east, a slow-rising ball of red flame that streaked the smoke-hazed horizon crimson.

"Esgallien will never fall," he said. "Though the wall be breached, though the statues of our long-dead heroes be toppled, though the great buildings of our city be levelled – Esgallien will endure, for the city is not, and never has been, any of those things. The city is our people, and what they love, and what they admire, and what they strive and hope for. That will endure in other cities and other places long after the streets of Esgallien grow green with grass. So, elùgroth, attack us if you must. Should you be victorious, know this: you might raze our city, but you can never extinguish the light that lasted a thousand years, and that light shines all the brighter as darkness gathers."

The elùgroth stood still. Silence deepened. No man on the wall moved or spoke. At length, Gar-galen bowed, and then without answer turned back to his host.

A murmur rippled along the battlements. Swords were struck against shields and a chant began.

Esgallien! Esgallien! Esgallien!

It swelled and rolled over the field below. The sorcerer did not look back. Instead, he gave a signal and the war drums of the elugs began to beat.

Aranloth sighed. "You've learned much since first I met you. And even if Gar-galen's host wins the day, you have robbed him of some of the victory he expected. He said as much when he bowed. Few are the times that I have seen him lost for words."

"Well, if he was lost for words, he'll make his actions speak all the more loudly." Lanrik looked over the enemy host. "See – he already orders the next attack."

A talnak horn sounded at that moment, and a mass of elugs surged forward.

"Yes," Aranloth answered, "but this time he will not attack with elugs only. Dark sorcery will follow in their wake."

The enemy raced toward them. In their trail came the archers. They all moved swiftly and with precision, regardless of their wild yelling. Yet something that Lanrik could not see properly moved amid the great host behind them.

The charge hit the wall, and the elugs threw up their ladders and ropes. Lanrik knew well enough what to expect. And the men were prepared for it. They could, perhaps, endure a siege like this for months. But this was no ordinary army that attacked them. It was vast, and growing, and seven sorcerers led it.

The elugs who survived arrow, spear and rock reached the rampart. There, they were cut down. And so swiftly was it done that they became resigned to their fate and fought without hope.

When the retreat sounded, those waiting their turn at the base of the wall receded like an outgoing tide and left their brethren atop the wall to die. As a black wave they rolled back to the host, but something was now visible in the open space that they left behind.

A portion of trunk from a massive tree, one that had grown for centuries and been felled in some dark valley among the hills and drawn here with immense effort, lay on the ground. Its girth was some ten feet. Its length fifty. The bark was stripped away, and the root and crown ends removed. But the exposed timber was not pale as it should have been. It was soaked in blood that turned it black. And great bands of iron clasped it like claws, and from the bands hung chains, and the metal of each link was as thick as a man's arm.

Each of the heavy chains was held by several lethrin. With a great heave, a hundred of them hauled in unison and lifted the log. As it came off the ground, Lanrik saw the near end clearly. A foot-thick cusp of iron was fitted tightly around it and held in place by metal bolts.

The enemy had built a mighty battering ram. Soaked by blood, it would be slow to catch fire. Massive, it would test River Gate as it had never yet been tested. Capped by iron, the wood would not split or shear on impact.

The elug war drums rumbled. The lethrin walked slowly ahead. Behind, in a dark wedge, came the elùgroths.

The lethrin gathered speed. They began to trot. At the head of the ram, the dull iron cap now flickered. As the lethrin drove it forward, the light flared into a sizzling green flame, bright but sickly, the hue of putrescent wounds and rotted meat. It formed a circle, with three slanted lines in its center: the drùgluck sign of ill omen.

The elùgroth wedge halted. Lanrik thought they would attack the gate. Instead, they pointed their wych-wood staffs at the tower where he stood. Gar-galen, it seemed, wanted to kill him. Or Aranloth. Or, more likely, to distract the lòhren from helping defend the gate from the sorcery being unleashed upon it.

Aranloth stepped to the edge of the battlement. He raised his staff. From the wedge, the same sickly green light as lit the ram, flashed in a bolt of lightning that sizzled through the air.

A dome of silver light flared. Aranloth stood in its center. The two powers of elùgai and lòhrengai met with a blinding flash. A crack of thunder sounded. Men reeled. Aranloth staggered back. The elùgroths fell and sprawled to the ground, all save Gar-galen. A mighty crash filled the air. It was not sorcerous thunder, but the ram smashing into River Gate.

A tremor ran through the tower. Wicked green light flared from below, yet blue fire contended with it. But on the dawn of that dark day fate was stronger than lòhrengai. The ram, prepared overnight, laden with dark sorcery, wielded by inhuman strength, smashed the gate thrice, and on the third blow struck it down in screeching ruin.

Atop the battlement Lanrik heard it, and he felt the footsteps of doom. Yet no faint heart was his. Gathering a score of men to him he raced down the tower stairs. Aranloth ran with him. No more sorcery would be expended on the walls. A breach was made at the gate, and the entire force of the enemy, elugs, lethrin, Azan and elùgroths would drive against it.

They raced down through the dark of the tower, and then into the open. A hundred of Esgallien's finest axemen stood guard. At their head were Erlissa and Aratar.

The lòhren's staffs flickered with light. Just before them was the second gate, built on the inner end of the killing tunnel.

The passageway was not dark as normal. Wicked green light filled it. In that eerie glow Lanrik saw the ram, propelled forward over the rubble of the first gate by lethrin. Immune to arrows shot through the killing slots, hindered little by oil and fire, they drove the ram onward. Behind, several sorcerers stood. Gar-galen was first among them.

Flame sprouted from their wych-wood staffs. The ram smote the gate. Erlissa and Aratar strove with all their might, weaving blue lòhrengai among the gate bars. To their help Lanrik and Aranloth sought to go, but the axemen were in their way and no path could be found in time.

With a boom and crash the gate splintered. The great ram tumbled forward onto the Hainer Lon, there to rest on the cobbles. A wreck of metal was about it; its dark surface smoldered.

Erlissa and Aratar dove to the left. The lethrin released their chains and hefted their maces. The axemen charged.

A furious battle started. Axes flashed. Maces smote. Sorcerous light streaked through the air, and lòhren-fire answered. All hung in the balance, but only for a moment.

Swiftly elugs joined the fray, darting in and out among the larger lethrin, pouring through the killing tunnel and flooding onto the Hainer Lon.

Many of the axemen were slain in their valiant defense against a foe greater than they. Reinforcements came, but ever the enemy pressed forward and the battle pushed back along the Hainer Lon.

The ranks of the enemy swelled. The southern army was inside Esgallien, and nothing would throw them out. And the fighting continued.

Lanrik and Aranloth were free to act, for many of the defenders that had been ahead of them were now dead. The enemy came on. A wave of them surged forward, separating him even further from Erlissa. He saw her in combat with Gar-galen. She was pressed hard, for Aratar was out of sight, stricken down somewhere and trampled beneath the boots of the enemy, and two other elùgroths joined forces against her.

For a second their eyes met through the host of enemies between them, and he saw the recognition of death in her eyes. The enemy seethed ahead, and she was lost from sight.

A moment Lanrik paused. The masses of the enemy lay between him and the girl that he loved. Grief struck him as a blow. The strength drained from his arms. He bowed his head, and hope died in his heart.

But something stirred within him. It rose through his body and flared like sudden fire in his eyes. The darkest hour of his life was upon him, but in that moment he knew that even without hope, in the face of certain death, yet still would he fight. He would defy the world if he must to reach her.

The sword of Conhain felt suddenly light in his hand. He swung and stabbed and spun among the enemy in a dance of death so furious, so strong in its onslaught that it made even the lethrin reel before him. Yet even as they parted they closed ranks again behind him, and Aranloth, who followed close in his wake.

Spattered by gore, his sword dripping blood, he came to Erlissa. He saw her, lying on the ground, trying to stand. But Gar-galen towered above her. One booted foot pinned down her hand that held the staff. The other rested heavily on her chest.

The elùgroth slipped a black dagger from his cloak. It was a wicked blade: curved, reeking of dark sorcery and filled with ancient malice that even Lanrik sensed. The overwhelming presence of the elùgroth smote him, yet Lanrik did not hesitate. With a single stride he was there.

Gar-galen saw him come. Green light flickered along the wych-wood staff. He pointed it at Lanrik, but the great blade of Conhain cut faster than light. One moment the staff was between them, the next both staff and the severed hand that still gripped it flew to the side.

194

Gar-galen screamed. Lanrik struck again. This time he stabbed, and the point of the blade drove into the elùgroth. Lanrik did not stop until the very hilt pressed against the sorcerer's body.

One moment they looked into each other's eyes. One moment they stood still amid the roiling battle. And then the life went out of Gar-galen. He toppled, and Lanrik withdrew his sword.

Lòhren-fire flared and the other two elùgroths perished in a blast of white fire. The elugs streaming in through the gate swerved away, but they did not stop coming.

Lanrik looked around. The three of them were caught amid the enemy host. There was no way back whence they came. There was no way forward through the gate. An alley opened to their left, and swiftly Lanrik did what he must. He stooped down and took Erlissa in his arms. He turned to Aranloth, but the lòhren was moving too. He despoiled Gar-galen's corpse of its black cloak. And then they ran into the narrow lane.

Because of fate, chance, good luck, or perhaps even the enemy's fear of them, they were not followed.

The noise of battle receded, but the triumphant note of the elug war drums did not.

Lanrik put Erlissa down on her feet and looked in her eyes.

"Are you all right?"

Erlissa rubbed her wrist. "I suppose. Just as well that you came when you did … I never thought to see you again. How you managed to reach me, I just don't know."

Aranloth grunted. "He did it with some fine sword work – but mostly he did it by force of will. Few are the men that have slain an elùgroth, Halathrin blade or no."

"We've come a long way together," Lanrik said. "I wasn't going to let a handful of the enemy and a pasty-faced sorcerer get between us." He looked back over his shoulder, but the alley was still empty. "The question is, what do we do now?"

"What will the *army* do?" Aranloth asked.

"The men will stream from the walls now that the gate is breached. They'll retreat to Conhain Court. After that …" he shrugged.

Erlissa gave him a weak smile. "They must think you're dead, you know."

"Probably," Aranloth agreed. "And that Conhain's sword is lost as well. If we're to give them any sort of hope at all, we must get back as soon as possible."

Lanrik ran a hand through his hair. "It'll take a long while though. We'll have to go by the back streets to avoid the Hainer Lon. The enemy will drive up along its length until they reach the center of the city."

Aranloth closed his eyes and thought, but not for long.

"That'll take too much time."

"Probably, but there's no other way."

"There is, though. You said it yourself. The enemy will force their way up the Hainer Lon. That's the quickest way to where we want to go as well, and we must go with them if we're not to arrive too late."

"And how can we possibly do that?"

Aranloth gave no answer. Instead, he flung up the elùgroth cloak and placed it over his shoulders. The dark hood he took, and shadowed his face with it. Tall he stood, and grim; a figure of black menace, yet his staff remained white. But with a crack he stamped its end against the cobbled road. Lòhrengai flared, silvery white. It ran along the staff and leapt like a spark to the cloak, and then it leapt back to the staff. And the staff was become black.

Aranloth looked at the two of them. "You shall become elugs, and we will fly up the Hainer Lon, moving through the ranks of the enemy until we come to Conhain Court."

They did not argue with him, risky as the plan seemed. Certainly, the lòhren now looked the part of an elùgroth, but he and Erlissa must yet find elugs, and take their cloaks and curved swords. He knew that they would not look so convincing.

They moved along the alley and into other streets that traveled parallel to the Hainer Lon. They did not wish to go back anywhere too near the gates, lest someone was still there who might recognize them.

Soon they turned their feet back in the right direction. The noise grew swiftly loud. There were yells and screams and the shattering of stone. The enemy laid waste to the city as they went, yet its vanguard would be pressing Esgallien's soldiers backward.

They neared the Hainer Lon. Lanrik thought that they must try to lure elugs into a side street and there waylay them to obtain the disguise they needed, but that proved unnecessary.

The enemy streamed ahead, but at the sides of the Hainer Lon dead elugs lay in heaps. They were not having things all their own way, for Esgallien's soldiers ceded the ground reluctantly.

Aranloth strode out onto to the road. They stayed in the shadows of the alley.

The lòhren chose two corpses and took their cloaks and swords. The masses of marching elugs walked around him. If they wondered what he was doing, fear made them ignore it. No one questioned elùgroths.

Aranloth returned. He gave them the grim booty he had collected. If Erlissa felt distaste at wearing a blood-covered and filthy elug cloak, she did not show it.

"What of your staff," Lanrik said.

Aranloth answered. "I'll carry it. Better that an elùgroth carries two staffs than an elug one."

The lòhren did not wait for them. Time pressed. He strode onto the Hainer Lon, and sudden menace hung over him like a cloak. No one heeded the two figures who scurried in his shadow.

All around the enemy seethed and marched and shouted. From somewhere behind came the hateful sound of the drums, beating now within Esgallien itself. Ahead was the clash of blade on blade and the curses of the injured. Smoke was in the air, and laughter, wicked and cruel, drifted down shadowy lanes.

Aranloth strode onward. His hooded head turned neither right nor left. He paid no heed to anything, but the southern army saw him and stayed clear. Always a path opened before him, no matter how thick the ranks of marching elugs. And if the enemy thought there was something strange about the two followers, scimitars drawn, hoods up, who hastened in his wake, they said nothing for fear of drawing the elùgroth's attention to themselves.

Lanrik coughed. Smoke curled through the shattered windows of a house to their left, and he knew that soon the city would burn. No one would put out the fires, and the houses would be looted and torched until the city blazed.

He began to take each step with a weight of dread. Not only of discovery by the enemy, but also of the harm being wrought to the city.

He did not pause as he walked by the Hamalath. But he looked and he saw. The massive columns of granite were beyond the harm of elugs, but the intricate carvings on them were not. Already the enemy had defaced them. Hammer and mace had chipped them; shield and sword hilt had notched them. Worse would come.

The Merenloth was next. It was empty now, no longer a place for reasoned debate, for men who sought to understand the world. Only the voices of elugs would rise there now, harsh and cruel.

The Haranast followed soon after. There was no damage there; not yet, except for one thing: the stele commemorating King Conmur, who had ordered its building, had been pulled from the ground. But it had not been broken or discarded. Instead, it had been turned upside down and rammed back into its hole.

The Hainer Lon reeked of smoke. It burned his eyes. His hand clenched the hilt of his elug scimitar. Erlissa did not pause beside him, yet he caught a glimpse of her face beneath her hood. She was pale, and there were tears on her cheeks.

The Karlenthern was next. There he had watched Lathmai win the archery tournament of the Spring Games. Here many of the ancient stone benches had been ripped up, broken, and cast down. Lathmai's heart would have broken to see it now. Perhaps death had saved her from the sight.

Looking at the destruction of the city around him was like a knife in his heart. He thought that he should have felt rage, but he did not. Instead, despair settled over him: cold, bleak, and inescapable. All things would end, and he among them. Whether it was in the next few minutes, or tonight, or in fifty years, he too would go the way of Esgallien. Was there anything worth living for?

The army thickened. All about them rank after rank of the enemy came to a standstill. Aranloth whipped his staff against the shoulder of an elug, and the crowd parted for him. Lanrik and Erlissa followed close.

It was hard to tell where they were, with the smoke in the air and the massed ranks of the enemy blotting out the view around them, but he knew when they pressed close to Conhain Court. For some reason there was a pause in the fighting, and the sound of arms ceased. But the drums coming up from behind only grew louder.

They passed through the milling elugs. At length, they came to the front of the ranks. There was no fighting. But ahead, separated by a small gap, was Conhain Court. In its vast space the army of Esgallien had assembled, all who had made it here from the wall.

Piled in the gap between the armies were the corpses of the slain. Most were elugs, but there were many men also. Ahead, he saw the Lindrath and some of the generals, but now the moment of greatest danger was come. How to reach them without getting an arrow in the back?

Aranloth did not hesitate. He walked into the open space between the armies. Lanrik and Erlissa followed.

Yet the lòhren knew this was dangerous too. He held up one hand, palm out. And his voice, aided by lòhrengai, hissed across the gap.

"I would speak with your leader," he said.

The Lindrath stepped a few paces forward. Two generals hesitated and then joined him. They were not alone. A troop of archers set arrows to their bowstrings and shuffled closer as well.

A silence fell over both armies. Lanrik kept walking, his heartbeat suddenly loud.

They reached within a dozen paces.

"Hold!" cried the Lindrath. "That's close enough. "Speak, and be done. We have no trust for you."

Aranloth tilted his head. But said nothing.

Lanrik stepped to his side. The arrow points followed him. He did not speak either, but behind them noise grew and there was some sort of commotion.

Lanrik lowered his sword, but with his left hand made the sign of the fox, the sign that only a Raithlin would know.

For a moment, the Lindrath did not see it. When he did, his eyes widened, and Lanrik tilted his head so that his hood fell a little to the side. It was enough; the Lindrath recognized him.

Behind came a series of yells, and then an elùgroth strode forward.

"Wait!" the sorcerer cried.

The Lindrath did not hesitate. "Let them through!" he shouted to the archers. The generals looked at him in confusion.

But the archers did shoot. The elùgroth raced forward, wych-wood staff ablaze, and the arrows loosed upon him sizzled and smoked, turning to ash in the air. None touched him.

The ruse was revealed. Lanrik cast down his cloak, and Erlissa did likewise. They raced toward Esgallien's army.

Aranloth turned and faced the elùgroth. He too cast aside his disguise. He threw the walnut staff to Erlissa as she passed him, and then swung his staff through the air. The blackness upon it was flung off like drops of water until the wood gleamed white, as did his robes.

The elùgroth halted. He lifted his staff and a bolt of red fire sizzled at Aranloth.

The lòhren stood tall. White fire answered, and Conhain Court thundered. Glass shattered in several of the nearby buildings.

The elùgroth reeled back, but he was not done. Yet he had no chance to attack again. With a mighty thrust,

Aranloth stamped the end of his staff against the street. The earth shook. Buildings groaned. A great rumble went through the ground and the cobbles beneath thousands of boots buckled like a wave of water.

Nearby, houses collapsed. The elùgroth retreated. Where he had stood, a massive building tumbled in a ruin of stone and choking dust.

A barrier now lay between Esgallien's soldiers in Conhain Court and the enemy on the Hainer Lon, but it would not separate them long. Soon the enemy would clamber over it. Soon they would come in from the sides. Soon the men of Esgallien would be surrounded. Now they must act quickly if they were to live.

Lanrik turned to the Lindrath and the generals.

"The city is lost," he said. "We can stay here, to fight and die, or we can take the chance Aranloth has given us to escape. Follow me!"

The generals did not argue.

Lanrik drew Conhain's sword so that the men would know him. The Lindrath blew the talnak horn.

"To Gold Gate!" Lanrik cried. "And to our friends and family beyond them. Esgallien is lost, but they are not, and they will need us. March!"

And the army marched. One last look he had at Conhain Court from the rear of the ranks; one final glimpse of the statues of the kings, and last of all his gaze lingered on Conhain. The court was silent. No one was there. The enemy did not yet dare to ascend the rubble.

The statue of Conhain on his great warhorse was proud and valiant. The king held high the Red Cloth of Victory, which signified victory from defeat, courage from sacrifice, hope from despair. And that was how Lanrik would remember it.

Epilogue

The enemy pursued them. But they fought a retreat up and into the forested hills beyond Gold Gate. There, the Azan riders could not bring the advantage of their mounts to bear.

Down in the city fires burned unhindered, and elugs looted. It was a red sunset. All the sunsets for many days were so, for a great pall of smoke and ash filled the sky: Esgallien's funeral pyre was vast.

The Raithlin led the host along dim and hidden trails. On the fourth day, they ventured down onto the road again. There was no sign of the enemy. They still looted the city and reveled in their victory, and a great victory it was. Now, the way was opened to the rest of the north, and they would seek to conquer it.

Camarelon might be next. Or Cardoroth. But though the enemy had the victory, it was not complete, for many of Esgallien's soldiers survived. They would swell the ranks of another king's armies. And they would fight again. Most of all, the women and children of Esgallien survived.

They caught up with the exiled host near the Hills of Enorien. There, they looked down at the great camp one evening while snow fell and powdered the ground.

Lanrik, Erlissa and Aranloth stood on a rise by themselves.

"This much is good at least," Erlissa said.

"What?" Lanrik asked, raising his weary head from deep thought.

She pointed to the host.

"See! There are women and children. Many of their husbands, and their husbands to be, and their fathers, and their brothers come now to join them. They are alive, and that was you. You couldn't save the city. It wasn't fated, but you saved them, who otherwise would have perished."

Lanrik looked at them. His heart lightened.

"You could be their king, Lanrik," Aranloth said softly. "They would follow you. You could forge a new kingdom as once your grandsire did."

Lanrik looked at them again. They *would* follow him, that he knew. He fingered the hilt of Conhain's sword. A while he stood thus in thought, and no one spoke.

At length, he reached out and held Erlissa's hand.

"Perhaps I could be a king, but they will find homes in already established realms, and it will be better for them. Besides," he paused and squeezed Erlissa's hand, "I have other places to be and other things to do."

A long while they stood in silence while the army marched down to reunite with their friends and family, but Lanrik gave no further orders. None of the three of them went down.

The sun set. Darkness grew. Fires flared to life in the camp, and song filled the air.

Aranloth stood unnaturally still. When he spoke, his voice came from faraway, for he described a vision not seen by eyes.

"From their midst a great hope shall come. One will be born that otherwise would not have lived, for if Esgallien did not fall, his parents would never have met. He will rise to power, and the south will learn to fear him."

Aranloth said no more. The vision was gone, and he sighed. Together, the three of them walked back over the rim of the hill and away from the camp. There the

Raithlin and their horses waited for them. They mounted and rode northward.

Thus ends *Blades of the Banished*. It brings the Raithlindrath series to a conclusion. Yet the growing power of the south imperils all of Alithoras, and more of the desperate struggle is told in …

KING'S LAST HOPE

Sign up below and be the first to hear about new book releases, see previews and learn of upcoming discounts. http://eepurl.com/Rswv1

Visit my website at www.homeofhighfantasy.com

Encyclopedic Glossary

Many races dwell in Alithoras. All have their own language, and though sometimes related to one another, the changes sparked by migration, isolation and various influences often render these tongues unintelligible to each other.

The ascendancy of Halathrin culture, combined with their widespread efforts to secure and maintain allies against elug incursions, has made their language the primary means of communication between diverse peoples.

For instance, a soldier of Esgallien addressing a ship's captain from Camarelon would speak Halathrin, or a simplified version of it, even though their native speeches stem from the same ancestral language.

This glossary contains a range of names and terms. Many are of Halathrin origin, and their meaning is provided. The remainder derive from native tongues and are obscure, so meanings are only given intermittently.

Some variation exists within the Halathrin language, chiefly between the regions of Halathar and Alonin. The most obvious example is the latter's preference for a "dh" spelling instead of "th".

Often, Camar names and Halathrin elements are combined. This is especially so for the aristocracy. No other tribes had such long-term friendship with the Halathrin, and though in this relationship they lost some of their natural culture, they gained nobility and knowledge in return.

List of abbreviations:

Azn. Azan

Cam. Camar

Chg. Cheng

Comb. Combined

Cor. Corrupted form

Duth. Duthenor

Esg. Esgallien

Hal. Halathrin

Leth. Letharn

Prn. Pronounced

Alar: *Azn.* A strain of horses raised in the southern deserts of Alithoras. Bred for endurance, but capable of bursts of speed. Most valued possession of the Azan people, who measure wealth and status by their number. In their culture, where a person on foot is likely to die between water sources, horse-theft is punished by torture and death.

Alithoras: *Hal.* "Silver land." The Halathrin name for the continent they settled after the exodus. Refers to the extensive river and lake systems they found and their appreciation of the beauty of the land.

Aranloth: *Hal.* "Noble might." A lòhren.

Aratar: *Cor. Hal.* "Ara(n)tar(an) – noble father." A lòhren.

Arawdan: *Esg.* A Raithlin. Brother to Arawnus.

Arawnus: *Esg.* A Raithlin. Brother to Arawdan.

Assurah: *Azn.* A renowned sword-smith of ancient Azanbulzibar, capital city of the Azan people. He was also adept at elùgai, and his work was sought by the rich and powerful of many nations.

Aurochs: The wild forebear of domesticated cattle. They are larger and more aggressive than their tamed descendants and prefer to graze and forage in swamps and wet forests. The "s" at the end of their name is both singular and plural.

Azan: *Azn.* Desert-dwelling people. Their nobility often serve as leaders of elug armies. They are a prideful race, often haughty and domineering, but they also adhere to a strict code of honor.

Brinhain: *Comb. Esg & Hal.* First element unknown, second "hero." A captain in Esgallien's Royal Guard.

Caladhrist: *Hal. Prn.* Kal-ath-rist. "Gold gorge." A valley north of Esgallien. Rich in gold and the source of much of the city's wealth subsequent to the depletion of closer alluvial deposits. Many others mined the valley through the history of Alithoras, including the Letharn. A dangerous place and believed by many to be haunted.

Camar: *Cam. Prn.* Kay-mar. A race of interrelated tribes that migrated in two main stages. The first brought them to the vicinity of Halathar; in the second, they separated and established cities along a broad sweep of eastern Alithoras.

Camarelon: *Cam. Prn.* Kam-arelon. A port city and capital of a Camar tribe. It was founded after Esgallien as the waves of migrating people settled the more southerly lands first. Each new migration tended northward. It is perhaps the most representative of a traditional Camar realm, while Esgallien is the most influenced by Halathrin culture.

Cardoroth: *Cor. Hal. Comb. Cam.* A Camar city, often called Red Cardoroth. Some say this alludes to the red granite commonly used in the construction of its buildings, others that it refers to a prophecy of destruction.

Careth Nien: *Hal. Prn.* Kareth nyen. "Great River." Largest river in Alithoras. Has its source in the mountains of Anast Dennath and runs southeast across the land before emptying into the sea. It was over this river (which sometimes freezes along its northern length) that the Camar, Duthenor and other tribes migrated into the eastern lands.

Careth Tar: *Cor. Hal.* "Careth Tar(an) – Great Father." Title of respect for the leader of the lòhrens.

Carnona: *Cam.* The Guardian of Enorìen. A creature of ùhrengai who has remained in her birthing lands.

Conhain: *Comb. Esg & Hal.* First element unknown, second "hero." Accounted the first king of Esgallien.

Conhain Court: The heart of Esgallien city. A large square, colonnaded on all sides, and containing bronze statues of all Esgallien's kings and queens.

Conmur: *Esg.* A king of Esgallien.

Crenel: The vertical gap on a battlement between merlons. The merlon offers protection, the crenel a gap through which missiles are fired.

Drùgluck: A pattern of three slanted lines, going from right to left and each one longer than the previous. Used by elugs as a warning to stay away from a place because it is a sacred area that serves as a gateway between the spirit and normal worlds. Such areas are used in ceremonies and invocations for help or retribution against enemies. It is believed that at certain cycles of the moon and seasons the barriers that separate the worlds are weakened and the gateway opens. Also marks a place where the effects of elùgai linger or where there is some unspecified but lethal danger. Often it signifies all three at once.

Ebona: *Cam.* A witch. A being of ùhrengai who has long since left her birthing lands.

211

Elùgai: *Hal. Prn.* Eloo-guy. "Shadowed force." The sorcery of an elùgroth.

Elùgroth: *Hal. Prn.* Eloo-groth. "Shadowed horror." A sorcerer. They often take names in the Halathrin tongue in mockery of the lòhren's practice to do so.

Elugs: *Hal.* "That which creeps in shadows." A cruel and superstitious race that inhabits the southern lands, especially the Graèglin Dennath.

Elù-Randùr: *Hal.* "Blade of the Shadow." An elùgroth leader. Formerly a lòhren.

Enorìen: *Cam.* The Eastern Hills. A land where ùhrengai runs strong. Protected by the Guardian Carnona.

Erlissa: *Esg.* A young woman of Esgallien. Also known as the Seeker. Now a lòhren.

Esgallien: *Hal. Prn.* Ez-gally-en. A city established by King Conhain. Named after the nearby ford.

Esgallien Ford: *Hal.* "Es – rushing water, gal(en) – green, lien – to cross: place of the crossing onto the green plains." A ford of the Careth Nien.

Exodus: The arrival of the Halathrin into Alithoras from an outside land. They came by ship and beached north of Anast Dennath.

Foresight: Premonition of the future. Can occur at random as a single image or as a longer sequence of events. Can also be deliberately sought by entering the realm between life and death where the spirit is released from the body to travel through space and time. To achieve this, the body must be brought to the very threshold of death. The first method is uncontrollable and rare. The second exceedingly rare but controllable for those with the skill and willingness to endure the danger.

Founding: The arrival of Conhain and his people near Esgallien Ford. This was nine hundred and fifty three years ago at the time of Lanrik's meeting with Erlissa and Aranloth.

Galenthern: *Hal.* "Green flat." Southern plains bounded by the Careth Nien and the Graèglin Dennath mountain range.

Gar-galen: *Hal.* "Star green." An elùgroth.

Graèglin Dennath: *Hal. Prn.* Greg-lin dennath. "Mountains of ash." Chain of mountains in southern Alithoras. The landscape is one of jagged stone and boulder, relieved only by gaping fissures from which plumes of ashen smoke ascend, thus leading to its name. Believed to be impassable because of the danger of poisonous air flowing from cracks, and the ground unexpectedly giving way, swallowing any who dare to tread its forbidden paths. In other places swathes of molten stone run in rivers down its slopes.

Grothanon: *Hal.* "Horror desert." The flat salt plains south of the Graèglin Dennath.

Guardian: A creature of sentient ùhrengai that preserves its birthing land.

Hainer Lon: *Hal. Prn.* Hiner lon. "Heroes way." The main thoroughfare of Esgallien.

Hakalakadan: *Azn.* A revered title among the Azan peoples.

Halathar: *Hal.* "Dwelling place of the people of Halath." The forest realm of the Halathrin.

Halathgar: *Hal.* "Bright star." Actually a constellation. Also known as the Lost Huntress.

Halathrin: *Hal.* "People of Halath." A race named after a mighty lord who led an exodus of his people to the continent of Alithoras in pursuit of justice, having sworn to redress a great evil. They are human, though of fairer form, greater skill and higher culture. They possess an inherent unity of body, mind and spirit enabling insight and endurance beyond other races of Alithoras. Reported to be immortal, but killed in great numbers during their conflicts with the evil they seek to destroy.

Halls of Lore: Library of records maintained by lòhrens of the history, knowledge and wisdom of the nations of Alithoras. Accumulated over millennia and one of the treasures of Lòrenta.

Hamalath: *Hal.* "Sorrow joy." An open-air theatre where dramas of history, tragedy and humor are conducted. Derived from the Halathrin who built many. In Esgallien called simply "The Hamalath," as there is only one of significant size.

Haranast: *Hal.* "Horse race." A racetrack. Its form was derived from the Halathrin but the love of horseracing by the Camar predates the exodus of the immortals. A successful rider, or horse, could be more famous and better loved than tribal chiefs or kings. The stealing of a racehorse is punishable by death.

Headdress: A turban. Worn by the Azan people as protection from desert heat. Can be lowered in a sandstorm to protect the eyes and breath. Its color, and the manner in which it's worn signify military rank or social status.

Karlenthern: *Hal.* "Games field." The location of many events during the Spring Games and other athletic competitions during the year.

Lanrik: *Esg.* A Raithlin. Also called the Raithlindrath.

Lathmai: *Comb. Hal. & Esg.* "Joy and unknown element." A Raithlin. She was killed in service to her country.

Letharn: *Hal.* "Stone Raisers. Builders." A race of people that in antiquity ruled much of Alithoras. Only traces of their civilization remain.

Lethrin: *Hal.* "Stone People." Creatures of the Graèglin Dennath. Renowned for their size and strength. Tunnelers and miners.

Lindrath: *Hal.* "People lord." A shortening of Raithlindrath. Commander of the Raithlin organization.

Lòhren: *Hal. Prn.* Ler-ren. "Knowledge giver – a counselor." Other terms used by various nations include wizard, druid and sage. They take names in the Halathrin tongue as it is the language of lore among the learned of Alithoras.

Lòhren-fire: A defensive manifestation of lòhrengai. The color of the flame varies according to the skill and temperament of the lòhren.

Lòhrengai: *Hal. Prn.* Ler-ren-guy. "Lòhren force." Enchantment, spell or use of arcane power. A manipulation and transformation ùhrengai, the natural energy inherent in all things. Each use takes something from the user. Likewise, some part of the transformed energy infuses them. Lòhrens use it sparingly.

Lòrenta: *Hal. Prn.* Ler-rent-a. "Hills of knowledge." Uplands in northern Alithoras in which the stronghold of the lòhrens is established.

Mecklar: *Esg.* Was once a senior member of King Murhain's retinue. A traitor slain by Lanrik in single combat.

Merenloth: *Hal. Prn.* Mair-en-loth. "Words of power." A place for philosophical debate, reciting poetry and the chanting of bards. Derived from Halathrin practice. Often full to capacity during times of change. King Danhain, disguised as a bard, often frequented the Merenloth and chanted pre-founding lays passed down from his grandfather. After the performance he discoursed with the crowd to determine what the people thought of the king's rule. He sometimes changed his decisions after such debates.

Merlon: The vertical stonework on a battlement between crenels. The merlon offers protection, the crenel a gap through which missiles are fired.

Murhain: *Esg.* The current king of Esgallien. He was a younger son of the previous king and assumed the throne unexpectedly. Earlier in his life, he had attempted to train as a Raithlin but failed their vigorous standards.

Musraka: *Azn.* A shazrahad.

Nudaluk: *Cam.* A bird of the woodpecker family.

Otherworld: Esgallien term for a mingling of half-remembered history, myth and the spirit world.

Pattern-welded: A blade forged and reforged from bundles of iron rods that are twisted and beaten. This creates a flexible core to which a hard edge is added. The process produces superior, distinctive and sought-after weapons.

Portico: A covered colonnade, often at the front of a building.

Raithlin: *Hal.* "Range and report people." A scouting and saboteur organization. They derive from ancient contact with, and the teachings of, the Halathrin. Disbanded by the king of Esgallien, but founded anew by Lanrik and dedicated to the service of all Alithoras.

Raithlin motif: A trotting fox looking back over its shoulder. A half moon rides above the animal. Symbolizes cunning, stealth and boldness.

Raithlin crawl: A famous technique of stealth. It requires that the palms rest on the earth and the elbows remain tucked in to the body for support and silhouette reduction. The bodyweight is borne on the forearms and only one leg. The other is carefully brought forward in order to avoid making noise while moving.

Raithlin creed: "Our duty is to serve and protect. Our honor is to fight but not hate. Our love is for all that is good in the world."

Raithlin principles of concealment: The Raithlin believe the eye recognizes movement first, silhouette second and color last. Using these principles enables them to best determine how to remain unseen in varying circumstances.

Raithlindrath: *Hal.* "Lord of range and report people."

Raithlin Sign: A secret hand sign. The thumb pulls down both middle fingers, leaving the two outside fingers standing up to represent the pricked ears of a fox. The sign, invented by Conhain, symbolizes cleverness. If pointed to the ground, and formed by the left hand, it signifies that great danger is near.

Red Cloth of Victory: The highest symbol of courage and determination in Esgallien society.

Royal Guard: Bodyguards to Esgallien royalty.

Seven Devil Peak: A legendary peak in the Graèglin Dennath mountains - a holy place to the elùgroths.

Shazrahad: *Azn.* The Azan who commands an elug army.

Shurilgar: *Hal.* "Midnight star." An elùgroth. Also called the betrayer of nations.

Sorcerer: See elùgroth.

Spring Games: A series of athletic and skill-based competitions in Esgallien deriving from antiquity. Other Camar peoples also conduct the games, sometimes under a different name. Before the tribes diverged, they met at various sacred sites marked by standing stones. There, amid sporting games, feasting and trade, chiefs were chosen, disputes settled and ceremonies conducted.

Talgin: *Esg. Prn.* The "g" is hard as in "go." The Lindrath of Esgallien. Mentor to Lanrik.

Talnak: *Azn.* A large goat-like animal that survives and even flourishes in the most remote and inhospitable regions of the Graèglin Dennath. Its preferred habitat makes it perilous to hunt, but its horn is highly valued by the Azan people and used in ceremonial rites.

Tor: A hill rising up from the plains of Galenthern. Site of Lathmai's grave.

Ùhrengai: *Hal. Prn.* Er-ren-guy. "Original force." The primordial force that existed before substance or time, light or dark, life or death, good or evil.

War drums: Drums of the elug tribes. Used especially in times of war or ceremony. Rumored to carry hidden messages in their beat and also to invoke sorcery.

Witchery: A type of elùgai. Distinct from the common spell-craft and potion making carried out by some village healers.

Witch-fire: A potent attack of elùgai.

Witch-queen: See Ebona.

Wych-wood: A general description for a range of supple and springy timbers. Some hardy varieties are prevalent on the poisonous slopes of the Graèglin Dennath mountain range and are favored by elùgroths as instruments of sorcery.

From the author

I'm a man born in the wrong era. My heart yearns for faraway places and even further afield times. Tolkien had me at the beginning of *The Hobbit* when he said, ". . . one morning long ago in the quiet of the world . . ."

Sometimes I imagine myself in a Viking mead-hall. The long winter night presses in, but the shimmering embers of a log in the hearth hold back both cold and dark. The chieftain calls for a story, and I take a sip from my drinking horn and stand up . . .

Or maybe the desert stars shine bright and clear, obscured occasionally by wisps of smoke from burning camel dung. A dry gust of wind marches sand grains across our lonely campsite, and the wayfarers about me stir restlessly. I sip cool water and begin to speak.

I'm a storyteller. A man to paint a picture by the slow music of words. I like to bring faraway places and times to life, to make hearts yearn for something they can never have, unless for a passing moment.